Wings of Bamboo
Alas de Carrizo

A Collection of
Childhood Stories

by
Esperanza Zendejas

Ojo Por Ojo
Publishing
San Jose, California
2005

Published by Ojo Por Ojo
6280 Blauer Lane
San Jose, California 95135

Esperanza Zendejas 1952-

For information on special school discounts for bulk purchases, please contact
publisher or visit website: http://www.esperanzazendejas.com/

ISBN 0-9670467-2-6

1. Hispanic Culture 2.Mexican-American 3. Immigrant Experience
4. Education 5. Autobiography 6. Southwest 7.Mexico 8.California
9. Imperial Valley

First Printing February 2005

10 9 8 7 6 5 4 3 2 1

"Curiosity has its own reasons for existing"

—Albert Einstein

Dedicación

This reconstruction of my memories growing up in a poor but loving family is dedicated to my adorable grandchildren: Crystal (October, 2000), Silvino (November, 2001), and Esperanza (June, 2004). I hope these short stories provide you with the inspiration to excel in school, to respect others and to cherish the love of family. Writing these stories has re-ignited many heartfelt and warm memories of growing up in the company of my brothers and sisters, mother and father in a humble and happy home. Always know that you are dearly loved!

Introduction

The inspiration for the stories in *Wings of Bamboo* (*Alas de Carrizo*) dates back to my mother and father in the early 1900's. My father, Silvino, a poor man from a humble background, was born on January 4, 1913, the youngest son of six children. My mother, María de Los Angeles, was born on November 13, 1913, also one of the youngest of six in her family. Both of my parents were born in the small, mountainous village of La Yerbabuena, Michoacán, México. My mother was raised in a more sophisticated and economically established family. My parents were married on March 29, 1932. Within twenty years of marriage, my parents had ten children.

As tradition dictated in rural México, after my parents' marriage, my mother was welcomed into my father's family as an additional pair of helping hands to assist with the customary daily tasks. She immediately was given the traditional chores of tortilla-making, cooking, washing, raising children and feeding chickens. My mother forever reminded us that on her first day as a new wife,

1

she had to learn to grind corn into a soft masa (dough) kneeling behind the *metate* (volcanic flat stone used for grinding corn and other grains). There was no such thing as a honeymoon during this post-revolutionary and hungry epoch of México. There was little celebration time for this marriage during those years of hardship for poor families. The future, however, was good to this marriage of 69 years, which outlasted so many others.

My first recollections of my childhood in rural México are filled with memories of a happy family with an absent father. My mother was the adult in charge while my father worked as a *Bracero* (workforce of Mexicans hired by the U.S. in the 40's through the 60's) in *El Norte* (United States). By the time I was two, my father was able to send enough money to provide the needed food and clothing for the nine hungry children. With the *Bracero* money, my mother was also able to keep and feed the tame donkey and egg-laying chickens. Prior to this time, my brothers talk about the times of real hunger and true scarcity. During these times, people were not afraid of losing since they had nothing to lose.

During my formative years, I did not know that we were poor or that we lacked anything in particular. Our village was isolated and years away from having electricity or drivable roads. Our home, like the rest, did not have electric power or running water; instead, we used candles and an open hearth for warmth in our kitchen. The open flames for cooking were maintained by adding or deleting wood from the fiery hearth. In the night, the large, silvery moon provided the only source of outdoor light. Many bright fireflies floated in the air to create the magical evenings under the stars in our village.

Dry wood was stacked against the earthen hearth in our kitchen to fuel the flames for the daily cooking. My brothers were responsible for keeping dry wood next to the hearth. Over and over again, the old donkey would haul the uneven loads of sticks and small branches brought from high in the surrounding hills of *El Cerro Prieto, El Cerro de La Piedra de Los Lobos* and *El Cerro de La Cruz* (Black Hill, Hill of the Lobos' Rock, Hill of the Cross).

Our fresh drinking water came from the *ojo de agua* (freshwater spring). One of the freshwater springs was located downhill from our home. The drinking water was stored in large *cántaros* (clay narrow-mouth pots). These clay *cántaros* kept the water cool during the hot days. The *cántaros* with the slightest crack were no longer able to hold the fresh water. These were often used for grain storage or for the breakable, decorated piñatas.

Our bathroom was an outdoor shack located away from the main adobe house. The secluded outhouse sat high over an unkempt dirt path. A sophisticated sewer system was managed in a plain and simple manner by the pigs of the village. As a child, I was captivated by the curious but nonchalant pigs carrying off the excrement below.

Once inside the rustic outhouse, the obligated visitors saw a large

wooden box with three holes cut for the comfort of the bottoms of
the family in three different sizes. The smallest hole was for the
children, and the largest for the grownups. The first time I
heard the story, "Goldilocks and The Three Bears," the image of
the practical outhouse in our Mexican village came to mind.

In rural México, kernel-less cobs were used instead of the soft and
scented toilet paper that we find today by most commodes. During
our visits to the wild hills and mountains, small rocks were used
instead of the corn products. When possible, the outhouse was
avoided by all. The *bacinilla*, (chamber pot) made of heavy
porcelain, usually painted white, was found in the homes that
could afford this household bit of comfort. Most people were too
poor to have the *bacinillas* in their homes. During the morning
hours and long after the moon disappeared behind the mountains,
all of the *bacinillas* were emptied, rinsed and readied for another
busy night.

In those days I had no idea that cars could transport families.
Only large trucks with huge tires were seen struggling on the
uneven cobblestone and rock-filled roads. The trucks bounced
mercilessly back and forth, traveling at caterpillar speed. Often,
men with their large sombreros would jump out of the trucks to
remove volcanic pieces of rock and boulders from the path of the
vehicle. Quickly, the men would hop into the back of the truck
until more rocks blocked their passage.

Seldom were the sounds from radios, microphones or record

players heard in our village, except on festive days. The only sounds in our village came from humans or animals. The roosters were the most noticeable, since they were the noisy early risers. There was no need for the obnoxious sounds of alarm clocks, thanks to the help of these colorful, feathery animals.

Given that our village of La Yerbabuena is nestled against a mountain, the echoes from the sounds of the chattering people ricocheted from one end of the cobblestone streets to the other and from one corner of the village to the next. The familiar voices and sounds of people were always present in the village, like spirits roaming in the flowery air. The donkeys' "hee haw" cries were also loud and could be heard throughout the village and as far away as the hills.

As the candlelight mourned the approaching darkness, the coyotes waited high in the hills to begin their melancholic moaning and sorrowful cries to the moon. At night, only the flickering light from the candles made up the night glow coming from the adobe windows and wooden doors. For the most part, men, women and children lived peacefully in the village of La Yerbabuena, Michoacán, México.

Besides having a *milpa* (crop) in México, it was enough to own a skinny donkey, a couple of pigs and a few egg-laying hens. Owning pigs was like having money in the bank in those days. The pigs were fattened for a future butchering or for trading. Families that had corn could trade their goods for pigs. In our village, pigs were fattened for the annual fiestas, weddings and for market. Pigs were a known commodity.

In rural México, the chickens fed the hungry mouths of the large families, and the burro was burdened with carrying the fresh water, wood and people left and right. Although the burros were skinny, they were able to carry the large-bellied men with huge sombreros. The undernourished burro welcomed the large sombreros for the shadows they created on their hairy bodies. The shadows from the large, traditional sombreros provided man and animal the needed protection from the year-round, scorching sun.

The boiled squash and steaming corn cobs made for a festive meal, along with fresh dove wings fried in hot lard with green tomatillo (small green tomato) sauce. In other cases, a fried egg chopped into three or four pieces with fresh tortillas, onions and beans was enough for the large family. The fresh, squash blossom corn quesadilla was my favorite, especially hot and toasty off the *comal* (flat earthenware griddle used for cooking tortillas). The yellow, melted cheese-like blossoms between the crispy corn tortillas were a heaven-sent seasonal treat for the stomach.

I grew up in a strong Catholic family, praying and faithfully attending all religious services. The church in our village was built by my ancestors many years before I was born. The whitewashed, mission-style church faced directly west to the sunset view. The large, rustic wooden door greeted the beautiful colors of the warm, tamed sunset. At the last glimpse of sunset, the soft rays reached the feet of the altar, creating an unexplainable aura. It was as if a warm Navajo blanket draped the church just before the nightfall.

The tile roof of the adobe church was supported by long, rustic wooden beams crisscrossing high above the simple pews. As a child, I enjoyed watching the many doves and sparrows that attended the same services from the high, lofty square beams and adobe holes. The sparrows often built mud nests high up in the church between the uneven adobe edges. It was exciting to watch the sparrows flying from one side to the other with their beaks filled with mud and grass for their new home. The dark, fresh mud nests were a deep contrast to the old-fashioned whitewash paint job on the church walls.

Once the birds' nests were finished, my eyes often roamed to find the flying sparrows as they darted from one corner of the church to the other, sporadically feeding their young. You could not miss the fluttering noises coming from the tiny, stealthy wings of the birds. Regardless, the church welcomed everyone, including the variety of birds that made their nest heavens above the congregation.

Every time the church bells sounded to announce another religious event, villagers were alerted to the start time by the number of tolls. We all knew the bells called the villagers for the early-morning daily and Sunday special masses. Saturday masses were not part of the routine until years later. For most of the time, we never saw the priest's facial expressions, as he was expected to face the holy altar, speaking in the foreign language of Latin. In the evenings, the rosary was recited by the women and a scattering of a few faithful men. Most men paid their respects by holding their hats with their two hands in front of their belt buckles. The widows and the lonely women whose husbands and sons had departed to the United States were visibly filled with sorrow during prayer. Their singing was filled with lament.

My mother made sure that in our family all *Santos* (saints) were held in high regard. The *Santos* were stationed in several important locations, including the sacred part of our adobe home, the altar. At all times, our homemade altar was neatly decorated with starched, embroidered white homemade doilies and fading paper flowers leftover from the previous fiesta. My mother made it a point to keep the humble shrine dressed and decorated for whatever occasion. Often, fresh flowers took center-stage in front of the small statuettes. Several yellow, wax-burning candles were also positioned in different parts of the altar. The dressy Virgin of Guadalupe and Saint Joseph with a long stem of *nardo* (aromatic lily flower) in his hand were always situated in the center of the adorned altar.

The *Santos* seemed to join our celebrations when things went well, and we prayed to them for an *esperanza* (hope) of healing during times of much suffering. México was so hungry that prayer filled many of the stomachs during these times of solitude and gloom. The fervor of the people believed that religious miracles were only a prayer away.

During special times of the year, my mother made sure we played the roles required by the church festivities. For the children, dressing up like angels and learning how to remain motionless during the masses or for the rosary were exciting times. Many families, including ours, had bamboo-framed wings that were decorated with pretty *papel de China* (tissue paper) or covered with cotton to give the graceful angels a heavenly appearance. Brown, corrugated cardboard wings were also used when bamboo wings were not available. Once decorated, the bamboo wings were delicately hung on the shoulders of the young. The wings were tied with material lacing the skinny shoulders of the children. The children with wings on their backs were dressed in all white, a symbol of purity and humble offering.

There was much competition among the children for the best-looking angel wings and angel outfit in the small, mountainous village. The wings of bamboo looked authentic and sturdy behind the young children's backs. For me, these sturdy wings of bamboo were an important part of growing up. Dressing up as an angel provided the opportunities for my first formal socialization experiences outside the protected family structure. The bamboo wings also were a sign of importance in our small village. In those days, elaborate bamboo wings were somewhat of a status symbol. Often, the poor could not afford the cotton or pretty tissue paper to decorate the wings. However, everyone could own a set of bamboo wings, since the needed bamboo plants grew generously alongside the village river. My mother, happily, was able to purchase the special goods to decorate my wings, thanks to the *dólares* (dollars) that my father dutifully sent from the United States.

Every day except Sunday, I anxiously waited for Gabriel, our postman, to ride into village with the day's news from the outside world. Gabriel rode his thin horse much like a debutante emerging from nowhere to the excitement and cheering of the people. Gabriel and his horse were responsible for bringing the letters filled with dollars and news from their loved ones living thousand of miles away. The skinny horse's shoes made beautiful sounds on the cobblestones as the Mexican postal worker made his way to the village plaza. Children of all ages would follow the gaunt horse to the center of the plaza, where the names of the recipients of mail would be called out one by one. Everyone knew when families received letters sent by airmail to México. Most likely, an airmail letter from the U.S. included much needed-money. Our postman and horseman, Gabriel, was thus responsible for bringing renewed hope and joy to many people during the difficult times of poverty.

Thanks to my father and mother, to this day, I have never forgotten the enchantment created from dressing up like an angel with a pair of sturdy wings on my back. My mother decorated *las alas de carrizo* (the wings of bamboo) with so much ingenuity and affection. She always made sure that the wings were firmly tied to my back before I ran off to the church with a group of other angels. The thought of the angel wings on my back creates an unforgettable and special personal celebration.

When my mother was a child, her mother also dressed her up as an angel for religious celebrations. She also wore wings of bamboo for church events. Her father had crafted them for her. My mother always pointed to her shoulder and reminded us of how she had been painfully burnt when a candle accidentally lit the cotton on her wings. The flames quickly spread to my mother's angel dress, wings and hair. Her father's quick thinking put out the potentially dangerous flames. As a precaution, my mother always made sure I was never close to any lighted candles during our motionless roles as angels. She also made sure that my hair was in tight braids or ponytails before dressing me up in the angel outfit.

As children, we were given strict instructions to remain still while everyone in the church watched the back of the priest as he faced the altar during the mass. We were frozen at the altar until the priest finally turned to face the devoted congregation to give his final blessing of the religious celebration. I ventured to believe that my wings could also take me high above the faithful congregation.

Managing the motionless hour or so was an early expectation, usually successfully met. At one of these special angel assignments, I happened to have a runny nose. This event was during Christmas, and I played an angel next to St. Joseph. I remember

the funny fake mustache worn by the young girl playing the role of St. Joseph. My wet nose was in urgent need of attention.

Undaunted, I raised my angel outfit to wipe my nose clean with my slip beneath. For many years, my mother told this story with a whimsical charm. Without video cameras to record these special moments, families spent much time sharing past memorable incidents involving their families.

When not in use, our bamboo-wing frames hung along the kitchen adobe walls, waiting for the next angel season. I am proud of the special times when I wore *alas de carrizo* (wings of bamboo). More importantly, the experience of standing before several hundred villagers, while they listened to the mass, helped develop my character and confidence, from an early age. I had always hoped that the wings of bamboo would someday propel me high into the sky alongside the sparrows and doves.

At a certain coming of age, we were all expected to know the litany of *Santos* after praying ten *misterios* (mysteries) of the rosary. As the youngest of the family, I usually sat close to the commanding and stoic director of this event, my mother. Do not ask me what the *misterios* meant to me as a child; I did not know. I just remembered the repetitious "*ruega por nosotros, ruega por nosotros, ruega por nosotros*" (pray for us) of the litany. I only knew that the rosary was the time that we all came together, regardless of our differences during the day, and by the end of every rosary we were the happiest family ever to have lived on this earth.

When the time came to group together for the rosary, my mother acted like a proud hen counting her chicks and corralling all of us into our cozy and humble place before a homemade altar. With the grey beads of the holy rosary between her expert fingers, my devoted mother began to pray, expecting all of us to chime in our unanimous response with a Hail Mary, Holy Mary or an Our Father. The deep voices of my brothers drowned out the childish voices of my sister Blanca and me. Our ears were great at catching the sounds that varied from brother to brother.

After the ten Holy Mary prayers of the traditional rosary, the family sang together, requesting additional blessings for the sick or for ones traveling, or those in far-away places, like my father in the United States. Since none of us were great singers, on occasion, squeaky or base sounds came from our mouths, creating a snickering laughter during the rosary. We could not be caught laughing during the rosary. When one of us was caught, my mother slowly turned her head away from the altar toward us to find out who the "wise one" was. We all froze, as we pretended to not know of ongoing laughter or funny singing during the revered rosary. We all learned to read and adhere to my mother's non-verbal messages.

In our village culture, the religious singing was more for the women. My brothers frequently sang behind their teeth, hoping that no one heard them. There was constant chatter about the loud, female voices in the church choir. Everyone knew it was Matilde, the all-around faithful maiden and devoted churchgoer of our *Iglesia de la Virgen de Guadalupe* (Church of the Virgen of

Guadalupe). The same occurred among the congregation during mass, with the loud singing coming from the women and the soft-spoken tones coming from the men's side of the church.

Shortly after I turned seven, the five youngest of nine in my family, along with my mother, immigrated to the Golden State to join our father in the distant country of America. Our first trip to America was by the Mexican railways, traveling from Zamora, Michoacán to Mexicali, Baja California. My father was a legal resident of the United States when we joined him in California's Imperial Valley. Prior to this, he had been part of the contracted labor plan known as the U. S. Government Bracero Program. He had also worked as an undocumented alien in a dairy located in Holtville, California.

My father received the help from his bosses to successfully immigrate us to the United States through a family sponsorship. The oldest siblings were no longer considered "children" and thus could not qualify to immigrate with us under the same petition. To this day, I am still perplexed that once children turn twenty-one years of age, they are no longer considered part of the family for immigration purposes by the United States. This policy projected a harsh reality, unsettling to the fabric of our Mexican culture, where children, no matter what their age, are always considered part of the family. In many families, including ours, the young live alongside the old. Old and young, living and dying are closely connected through the entire lifespan in a Mexican family; ours was no different.

Introduction

Back in our Mexican village, no one would ever have imagined that our family would be fully immersed into the melting pot of the United States. No one would ever have guessed that our future home would be in the middle of a colorful desert, criss-crossed by hundreds of canals carrying fresh water from the Colorado River for crop irrigation. The desert of the Imperial Valley was decorated by lines of the planned canals of all sizes, bringing life to this sun-drenched land. This desert, cradled between the Chocolate Mountains to the northeast and Mount Signal to the west, is one of the driest regions in southern California. Growing up in the Imperial Valley was a feast of opportunity and truly a blessing for all of us, where many lessons were learned.

Our new home was vastly different from that in our Mexican village. A most noteworthy difference was the one-hundred-degree summer heat. Our entire family made do with what we had and where we lived, and the summer heat became tolerable for a child of a happy family. The kind people of the Imperial Valley welcomed our family with open arms. Much of the furniture was given to us by those friendly people who welcomed us to the "Land of the Pioneers."

In the late sixties, most of my brothers and their families left the Imperial Valley for a short time, but for some strange reason, the pull of the sweet Colorado River water brought them back to the Winter Salad Bowl of the United States.

Like many immigrants before us; we found that our coming to the
United States was not without worries, sacrifice and suffering. Life
is seldom easy for immigrants, and ours was no exception. Our
early life experiences in the new country were simplified by our
parents' determination to keep us together as one happy and self-
sufficient family. Just like the beads woven together in a special
order for the rosary, my mother and father made it a point to keep
us as close together and as orderly as possible.

My father did not make much money to support the large, hungry
family. Therefore, everyone worked in our family, including my
sister and me, but my mother worked the hardest of all. She rose
before the first light and finally rested after everyone was secured
in their beds.

For many years, my mother had raised us alone, while my father
worked in the fields in the United States, visiting México only for
short periods of time. Finally, in the early sixties, our parents were
reunited, adding to the richness and bonding of our family. We all
knew we were extremely fortunate to be together growing up in
America, and proud of our Mexican roots. We were blessed to be
united. We had known of sons, fathers and husbands who had
ventured to foreign lands, never to return by choice or fate. This
was perhaps the saddest migration legacy being left in the minds
of the people.

My mother inspired the belief that someday, our dream would
come true when being together was stronger than the challenges

that we all faced growing up away from our father. Being raised in a different culture, a different country with a different language would be made simple, thanks to our mother's determination. My mother never gave up what she wanted for all of us. She also made it a point to demonstrate a spirit of resilience, never quitting even when the toughest challenges confronted her.

I lovingly recall my mother's spirit during the time when we lived in the dry, hot California desert. My mother was used to being surrounded by calla lilies, year-round *noche buenas* (poinsettias), *malvas*, bougainvillea, pomegranate trees, *chayote* vines and chrysanthemums, along with other deep-green succulent plants, foliage and flowers. The traditional hanging plants in old tin containers, contrasting with the dark adobe walls, were a common sight in México.

To the surprised amazement of all of us, my mother took it upon herself to desalinate the California desert ground surrounding our home to grow her flowers of bright colors in a short period of time. The struggle and effort to force the salted desert ground to produce beautiful, bright-colored blooms was an awesome undertaking, solely accomplished by my mother's relentless perseverance and belief that she could do it. Once again, she showed us all the strength in believing.

My mother was a creative thinker and an artist. She designed nativity scenes in her mind and developed her ideas into beautiful, miniature holiday setting. The nativity set always turned out perfectly, as if it had been designed from a drafted, detailed plan. During these times in the Imperial Valley, we were so poor that we could not afford any market-type glue, so my mother mixed flour and water and cooked the ingredients, making *engrudo* (white paste). This paste worked wonders in holding paper and material together. After the use of the sticky mixture, our hands felt stiff and dried up. My mother had that special talent to form things from mental pictures into actual, fascinating projects that always amazed the entire family.

The Spanish saying *"panza llena, corazón contento,"* (full stomach, happy heart), rang true in our family, thanks to my mother's cooking skills that filled the house with unforgettable aromas of cumin, garlic, cinnamon, onion, sizzling lard and hot oils to add to the lingering flavors. She patiently cooked all day long when we were growing up. As the yellow bus dropped us off in the late-after school hours, my mother waited with pots of cooked, chicken-based rice, dessert and other goodies to fill our anxious stomachs with real Mexican food.

Our palates never got used to the room-temperature hot dogs or bland pear purees served at school. The unforgettable, spicy smells of toasting peppers over the fire and the smell of refried *frijoles* (beans) in hot, dancing pork lard have lasted in both our stomachs and hearts. Today, at every familial gathering, we warmly remember the memories of my mother's fresh "from scratch" delicious cooking and the unforgettable pride she took in ensuring a certain contentment with regard to our meals.

Not everything that my mother prepared in the kitchen was popular with me or my family. However, my mother had our best interest in everything she did. She wanted my sister and me to be strong and smart, not to be weaklings when it came time to our studies and our playing. Because of my father's habits of swallowing raw eggs with a squirt of lemon before work, my mother wanted us to do the same. During his *Bracero* days, my father did not have my mother to cook for him, like many Mexican men in the same situation; he would gulp down the raw chicken eggs for breakfast instead.

Every morning, two or three cups waited on the table for us to grab and tilt against our lips for a slimy journey to the base of our stomachs. Once we learned how to manage the two raw eggs, the sunny yolks with slippery transparent whites and lemon ended in the hollow of our stomach. It took some time before I could swallow the two eggs at once. The egg white caused me the most trouble. As much as I liked the feathery chickens, I really did not have a fond taste for their raw eggs.

Reluctantly, I learned to swallow one raw egg at a time. At first, my throat would want to shut tight. After one egg slid calmly down my throat, my mother would crack the second egg while she watched every second to make sure that her orders were followed. As the raw eggs left the cavity of our mouths toward the stomach, it always felt as if the eggs wanted to make a "u-turn" back to the serving cup. Once the second egg was cracked, she squeezed lemon on the yolk and added a pinch of salt.

To avoid early disgust, I tried to mentally concentrate only on the lemon and salt. I made a purposeful effort to forget about the raw egg. These egg-swallowing experiences were way before any findings were publiclly reported on the high cholesterol found in egg yolks. My mother promised that the raw eggs would make us strong and capable of anything we wanted to do. She was right!

As part of her agenda to help us become stronger, my mother purchased *jarabe* (a type of syrup with vitamins sold in México). She also made the girls drink a cup full of this vitamin *jarabe* before we hopped on the school bus. She indicated that this *jarabe* would make us strong and smart. The *jarabe* had a similar taste to the cough medicines sold over the counter. For unknown reasons, the girls were considered weaker and in need of the nutritional support. My mother did not realize that America would offer a more varieties of nutritious foods than our Mexican village's limited menus of beans and corn.

My mother was not at all a procrastinator. She made sure that we all knew she meant business when she gave some sort of direction. She always asked us if we wanted things done when *"San Juan baje el dedo"* (Saint John brings his finger down). As a child, I really did not know what she was trying to say with her Saint John metaphor. Actually, she was trying to tell us that things never got done if we waited until Saint John brought his finger down; that could never happen because Saint John is always depicted with his finger pointed toward heaven, and statues do not move.

My mother made a lot of sense when it came to getting things done. Her engaging personality was contagious. Most importantly, she instilled the life-long commitment to the unity of our family. She wanted us to be proud of whom we were and of the deep and beautiful roots we brought to the United States. In the marrow of our bones, we all are still one proud, Mexican-born family with love, affection and dedication for America, thanks to the teaching of our mother, María de Los Angeles Gil de Zendejas.

My father, Silvino, is a voracious reader and, to this day, still reads one or two daily newspapers in English. His learning to read in English perhaps created a strong desire for his youngest to excel in education. His dream was that we all would complete our education, but at the same time, he allowed room for personal career choices.

In order to make my father happy, we must make sure he has a newspaper or two handy. He would be part owner of the *Los Angeles Times* if he had invested in the stock market every time he purchased the ink news. Although he could read and understand English newspapers well, he never bragged about his knowledge, until we were old enough to be challenged by his superior base of information. However, he never made us feel put down in any fashion. My father's work ethic served him well in the United States. As we were growing up, he reminded us "*El que no trabaja no come,*" (He who does not work does not eat). Much to my father's credit, we were able to find the balance between the two neighboring countries. He helped us to understand the importance of honoring two countries and respecting their traditions and their people. He taught us to be well-versed in moving from one culture to another without difficulty or shame. More importantly, he taught us to look at life with a positive and optimistic perspective. His zest for life is still unmatchable.

While we were growing up, my father modeled for us the importance of looking out for *la familia* (the family). He was always looking out for his brothers and going out of his way to locate them wherever they resided. He drove us to unknown locations, asking people questions about his relatives until he found the particular family member. My father was an excellent and willing chauffer, driving many hours without rest until he reached his destination.

When I began driving, our father taught me to change the oil, spark plugs and basic flat tires. He taught me about the intricate carburetors. He wanted me to be ready for the long drives that I would eventually take two or three times a year to Michoacán, Mexico.

My father also played an important role in our transition to our new American home. His abilities and skills to mainstream and to encourage us to live up to our potential motivated all of us to excel in personal and professional ways. Early on, he encouraged all of us to respect our new homeland as if it were our own. As funny as it may have seemed, my father never allowed us to throw the smallest bit of trash or waste on the roads we traveled.

He felt this would be disrespectful toward our new country. My father has always shown a deep love for America, with a strong support for American patriotism. He expected no less from us.

All of us learned to admire and respect the ways and wisdom of our father. Our wonderful and loving parents kept all nine of us glued together by infusing solid values of respect and hard work. Hard work was modeled by both of our parents. These values, high expectations and their parental love and devotion to the family helped engage the best of two countries, two cultures and two languages. Growing up in the sixties, I found the thought of bridging two cultures and two languages to be a natural and simple process. My parents managed the cultural changes in such a smooth, natural and welcoming manner that everything became so normal and reasonable, as if it were meant to be all the time.

The one disconnect that perhaps has been more noticeable in recent years between our Mexican cultural roots and our American way of life is that of how we relax. I do not believe that as a family we had many opportunities to learn the art of relaxation. We spent much of our time working for a salary or towards a set goal. All of our vacations were focused and dedicated to visiting family in México. I do not ever remember going on vacation other than to visit our family in México. A day off here and there for my father would often turn into a drive to visit local family members. Our short family trips were to visit my brothers, sisters and an uncle in the agricultural town of Lamont, California. Until a few years ago, my parents continued visiting the family members residing away

from home.   Vacations and visiting family were commingled for
them and now for us.

Our parents insured that we learn to find the keys to make things
happen for ourselves, never giving up on each other and staying
together as one family. It did not matter if we were hundreds of
miles apart; the family harmony and unity remained. My mother,
in particular, often requested that no matter what happened, we
should always get along as a family. She did not want any negative
discourse to occur between and among her nine children. All the
Santos that watched us pray and grow together would be proud of
what values our parents inspired in all of us.

The wings of bamboo, from my own angel pageant days, provided
a sense of faith and belonging, a secured feeling of acceptance.
The imaginary wings of bamboo offered a security and a belief
that we could do anything we wanted. After we left México, I
never wore the wings of bamboo again. Yet the wings continue to
provide the confidence to excel in the simplest ways of life. I can
turn back to feel the firm support of the imaginary wings attached
to my shoulders generating a faith capable of moving mountains.

The effort to reconstruct history accurately is perhaps the most
difficult part of writing these personal stories of growing up in two
cultures, two languages, two countries and one loving family.
Sometimes we only remember what we are told happened, and
sometimes we can remember just a few glimpses of the past. More
often, we remember only those times that made a strong and

meaningful impression. Perhaps that is one reason why I have such fond memories of my childhood and adolescent years.

The following stories paint the picture of growing up in beautiful rural village of México and then moving to the United States. Our family's unity, our migration to the North and my first American friends are just a part of the mosaic of my life. The following stories are pieces of a picture that shows lessons learned and reflections of who I am today.

—*Esperanza Zendejas*

Grandparents

Antonio, Josefa, Donaciano and Valeria

I have only fond memories of my dear grandparents. They all fed my curiosity with their ways and words. My maternal grandfather, Antonio, was a wise man with a multitude of talents. He was well-known among the indigenous people of Michoacán for his pyrotechnic shows. He used crude gun powder packed into sliced bamboo shoots for the colorful fireworks displays lighting the night skies during the religious fiestas. Bulky wooden barrels rested under a Mexican tile roof next to his flowering garden and fruit trees. Inside the barrels, large river rocks tumbled as the work began. We sat and turned the barrels while the large smooth rocks pounded the ingredients to make the unsophisticated gunpowder into a smooth, sand-like texture.

My talented grandfather was extremely careful and made it known to his family that gunpowder was not something one should mess with. The distinct smell of gunpowder was as fascinating to me as the colorful, dynamic shows that he proudly produced for the fiestas of all the surrounding villages and towns. My grandfather kept a watchful eye on his dealings with gunpowder. He was very intelligent and a man ahead of his times.

My grandfather, Antonio Gil, a stocky man, always wore a stylish, German-type homburg hat instead of the wide-brim, woven hats worn by most peasant men from the countryside. The fancy hats and dark, pressed jackets complemented my grandfather's prominence in the region.

He was also a beekeeper and a master of plant hybridizer. As his love for the plants flourished, he kept a fruit-growing orchard in the pueblo home. At any time of the year, fruit and flowers were abundant from the large orchard and garden. He would take us to his orchard, carrying a long stick with a sharp hook at the end. I remember pointing to the sweet limes camouflaged high in the beautiful trees, waiting for the ripe fruit to fall to the ground. On one special occasion, I clearly remember my grandfather telling me that I was going to grow up to be sharp and smart. I humbly treasured his words in my heart. As he pulled the small stick at the end of the long pole, it triggered the hook, plucking a sweet lime from high above. Before the fruit reached the ground, I caught it with my bare hands, provoking an unexpected, soft smile from my "*Apá* Antonio." He was pleasantly surprised by my agile and quick reaction in catching the falling fruit.

Many times during my elementary years, this incident with my grandfather stood firmly in my mind, whenever I felt like an "underdog."

My grandfather sold the beeswax for the homemade candles that the locals bought for their altars and religious celebrations. He also sold the golden, orange-blossom honey in the small town. My grandparents' *casa* always smelled different from our corn-smelling home in the rural, mountainous village. My grand-father's home had varying aromas, depending on the cooking or the garden activities. The unique smells of gunpowder and of serrín (sawdust), followed by the fragrant kitchen odors of boiling *guayabas* (guava fruit), were often present at the home of my grandparents. Some of the rooms were filled with the fragrance of fresh flowers or the aroma of burnt wax left over from the candle light of the night before.

The calla lilies, roses, chrysanthemums and hibiscus flowers were abundant, as were the bees seeking the sweetness of the year-round blossoms. Even the chickens looked pretty at my grand-father's home. He also raised white, beautiful ducks, brown geese and *guajolotes* (turkeys). The pure-white animals were extremely attractive to me as a young, inquisitive child. The large duck eggs were enormous compared to the small chicken eggs at home.

My grandmother, Josefa, was an extremely creative and talented woman. In addition to my grandfather's dangerous work with gun powder, my grandmother used her skills in harvesting honey and wax combs, making and selling cheese, and growing flowers to make ends meet for the large family of mostly girls. My *abuela* (grandmother) was known as a woman of strong religious convictions. During the year, she spent many hours building miniature wooden houses for her future nativity scenes. These scenes also included small, Barbie-size wax figures; she sewed miniature costumes of real material to make them resemble a miniature village in Jerusalem during the birth of Jesus.

In my eyes, my grandparents' home resembled a "rich" *hacienda*, filled with shiny, dark wood furniture, a strange- looking record player and a radio. Looking back on these memories, I can now see the European influence in their home decor. Her large wooden bed and fancy mattress were adorned with the most beautiful cross-stitched and crocheted bedspread. To keep the bed beautiful and off-limits for the grandchildren, she hid straight pins around the edges of the quilt-like bedspread. Although we had no aspirations to jump on the soft-looking and elegant bed, it was obvious that my grandmother did not want anyone on her bed. When we visited my grandmother's home, we were politely warned about the pins.

Later on, my maternal grandmother, Josefa, reminded me of the woman in Grant Woods' 1930 painting, *American Gothic.* Her hair was always tucked in place in a well groomed bun hairpiece that she had made herself out of her own hair. Her symmetrical face was bold and unwavering.

Regretfully, we always felt like guests at our mother's parents' home. We were never allowed to mention these feelings out loud until many years later when we told the stories of growing up in a poor village and having grandparents who lived in a much better environment.

Grandparents

My father tells of herding mules for our grandfather's businesses. Early in the marriage, my father did not have the proper clout with his in-laws; therefore, he was given work befitting his lower status- herding the family mules. Perhaps we never really gave much importance to the fancy things that were absent in our adobe mud home in our small village. Overall, my grandparents' home was an exciting and interesting place to visit. My mother had so many fine memories of her father and mother and shared these with us all the time. More importantly, we loved our grandparents very much.

My father, on the other hand, came from a dirt-poor family who depended on the corn crop, squash, beans and the eggs from a few chickens for daily meals. Everyone in his family tended their milpas (cornfields) planted on the green hills of the mountainous village. My grandfather, Chano, died in the early sixties of Parkinson's disease. I always remember him sitting in his large chair taking in the morning sun. His blondish hair and his mustache glistened under the bright light. His sharp, hazel eyes were lost in the shade of his Mexican hat. His hands always trembled, as he pointed in the direction of the chickens darting in various directions on the nicely packed cobblestone yard. My grandfather enjoyed watching me chase the sneaky chickens with my four year-old, uncoordinated, curious hands.

My father's mother, Valeria, was a wise woman with strong indigenous facial features and long, dark braids hanging to her sides. Her high-cheekboned, happy face always reflected warmth and kindness toward us. My dear grandmother was a strong role model for me. She was a woman with a sharp eye for quickly analyzing people, with a unique manner of describing the way of life in the Mexican countryside.

Early on, my grandmother must have noticed my love of birds, long before I could understand my own affection for the feathered animals. My grandmother, Valeria, gave me a chicken that I kept until I left for the United States. *La Coqueta* was my friend and playing partner from the chicken coop to the earthen kitchen floor. When we left our small village, I vividly remember crying for *La Coqueta,* and hating to leave her behind. The funny chicken and I spent much time inside the chicken coop waiting for eggs to appear; I knew when this happened because some of the chickens made a fuss with their noisy attitude, anticipating the egg that softly appeared. Fortunately, I was the only one small enough to enter the chicken coop. This assignment added much to my confidence and abilities, as I was the only one able to complete the chore of fetching the breakfast or lunch eggs.

During our many trips back to México to visit our grandmother, I anticipated the arrival and the surprised look deep in her hazel eyes. It was the farewell that always turned emotional for all of us. It was difficult to see my father's pained face when he received my grandmother's farewell blessing. One by one, we all had to bow our heads to her petite level, so that her frail hands could reach out to honor us with her *bendición* (blessing); we could feel the touch of fondness and love on our forehead. Her touch was filled with lasting love. My grandmother Valeria was the pillar of our family. We all called her *Mi Amá Valeria*. I tenderly remember the aging and skinny hands filled with large, protruding blood vessels, whenever she began the last blessing, gently touching our forehead as the start of the treasured blessing. The special blessing was completed after the entire sign of the cross was made by us, followed by the kissing of the back of her soft, elderly hand. A choking silence prevailed as the tears flowed from every family member, quietly acknowledging that this might be the last time we saw her in life or that she would see us. The sorrowful farewell was always a powerful dose of reality and knowledge that every migrant family at some point or another had unexpected tragedies in and or out of México. For many years, my grandmother assured us that it was going to be the last time she saw us. Because of her soft and teary words, the *bendición* always hurt so profoundly and at the same time provided my heart with a deep sense of love and compassion.

As time passed, her fragile bone structure and large hump on her back made it difficult for her to move. Because of the hard life and osteoporosis, her frail body frame had significantly diminished. For many years, she moved throughout the village using a wooden cane to support her trips to the church to pray the rosary or to attend the mass. Someday, I hope to use the same cane to move around when my frail body becomes slow and weak.

Both sets of grandparents were deeply saddened when we departed to the distant lands of American. Later, my mother's parents left central México to move to the border town of Tijuana, México. My father's parents remained in La Yerbabuena. My grandfather Chano (my father's side) passed in the early sixties. My father was devastated that he could not travel to attend the funeral due to the lack of funds to pay for the trip. To this day, he regrets not borrowing money to make the trip to his father's funeral.

From the time my father and mother returned to México in the early 80's, they took full responsibility in caring for my grandmother Valeria until her final breath. My mother took it upon herself to care for her mother-in-law in a very special and loving manner. Her passing at 101 years of age was a painful experience for me, as I had lost my special support and comfort during difficult times. She died in the quiet of our humble home in Mexico.

My mother's parents are buried in a Los Angeles suburb cemetery. My grandparents on my mother's side were people of great talent and creativity. My father's parents are buried in the village cemetery, El Nopal Manso, in La Yerbabuena, Michoacán. Both of my father's parents were country folk with an inspiring and powerful belief in the simplicity of family unity.

My brothers, sisters and I have adopted personalities and ways that were first introduced to us by our grandparents. Having the variety of backgrounds, experiences and levels of socialization that both sets of grandparents offered to us provided us a firm and clear understanding of who we are and where we come from. In retrospect, we owe our ancestors a great deal of appreciation for leaving the path clearly defined by our culture, our language and our ways. Our grandparents modeled the respect for their loved ones and their siblings during the time that we were growing up. Our parents followed in leading our family with the strong values and attitudes about people, expectations and most important, the knowledge of knowing that life is generally peaceful. Today, to honor our ancestors is to honor our culture and our language.

My Brothers, Sisters and I
María Elena, Gustavo, Rodolfo, Maria del Refugio,
Alfonso, Luís, Hector, Blanca and Esperanza
1933-1952

My parents' first child was María Elena, born in July of 1933, followed by a son, Gustavo, born in April of 1935. Today, many would say that the first two children born to my parents were the prettiest and cutest of the family. These two members of the family would neither deny these favorable opinions nor suggest that others are more attractive than themselves. In many of the early pictures of the family members, my sister María Elena exudes constant confidence in her dainty looks by resting her hands on her hips with her pretty legs slightly bent at the knees, one toe always pointing toward the camera lens. She was always humbly fashionable, as we could not afford more. She was never seen without her lips shaded in hot red. In addition, everyone in our family knew that she had many admirers of the opposite sex. To this day, she remembers all the names of her beaus and many of their attributes or lack thereof.

By the time I was in *parvol* (kindergarten), my sister María Elena lived in a fancier world with my maternal grandparents, in a nice home with important-looking pieces of furniture and real beds. Visiting her was like visiting the city, a place of fancy things. María Elena also introduced me to México City. The trip to the city was a colorful and noisy experience. In México City, the wonders of electricity, running cars and flushing toilets sparked much of my curiosity. Instead of wooden outhouses, pigs and donkeys, large colorful buses and honking Volkswagen taxis lined the noisy streets. It was my first time seeing children on shoes with wheels, moving smoothly across the flat surface of cemented patios. We could never have done this type of gliding on the uneven cobblestone streets and dusty paths of our small village at La Yerbabuena, Michoacán, México.

In México City, my sister also arranged my first visit to an indoor theater. Back at our village, movies were shown outside on a large, graying and unattractive canvas pulled tautly at the four corners by plain rope. We each had to bring our own chairs to the outdoor show. At the outdoor movies, loose dirt provided a great opportunity for fleas to crawl inside our shoes and socks. Back in México City, when I was told we were going to the movies, I picked up my own chair and began walking out with it until I was told that the theater had its own chairs. I was just doing what I was expected to do in our village when the black and white Pedro Infante movies were shown. I had never seen an indoor theater or one with its own chairs. I remember everyone laughing at my unpopular, country folk culture that seemed too slow for city life.

Gustavo, sometimes referred to by others as "Gus," is the "horse whisperer" of the family. His life is never complete unless his saddle and faithful horse are at arm's reach. He would prefer to confess his mortal sins to his loyal horse than to a priest. Often, his nomadic jobs kept him and his family in distant locations. Gustavo has the million-dollar smile envied by many. His fine nose, blue eyes and graying mustache form the perfect image of the cigarette ads as the rugged "Marlboro Man" on his horse next to a campfire's black silk smoke. He believes that "horses are truly man's best friends;" no one will ever convince him otherwise. Gus has always worked with horses, managing their personalities.

At a very young age, he would proudly parade me through our village on a bare back mount to show off the once bronco horse finally tamed like a house pet. He does not forget the major scolding he received from my mother after one of his tamed horses bounced me to the cobblestone street after the horse changed his character for a brief moment. The scar left by the unexpected fall was a constant reminder of Gustavo's risk-taking approach with horses and his ways of showing off his equine skills.

My mother credited some of Gustavo's convincing and determined personality and his great health to his early adventures and work with horses. He is known for having the courage to drink donkey's fresh, warm milk during times of scarcity. During my early years, Gustavo spoiled me and filled me with the needed childhood attention of which all little girls dream. In some way, he filled in for the long absences of my father.

After Gustavo came Rodolfo, born in June of 1937. Rodolfo, better known as Rodo, inherited the "green thumb" from my grandfather. He is the best at growing beautiful plants from simple seedlings. He always had a way with dogs when I was growing up. He enjoyed tossing small bits of warm corn tortilla over his shoulder to feed the skinny-boned dogs competing for the airborne snack. After each silly jump to catch a morsel of tortilla, the dogs sat and impatiently waited like a groom at the altar when the bride is late. The airborne food was always an amusing sight to the young eyes in the family-oriented kitchen.

My fondest memories of my brother, Rodo, are of his occasional visits to our home in Imperial Valley, on his way back to México to visit his own children. He showered me with his pocket change of quarters, dimes, nickels and pennies--truly a treasure for me, since paper dolls and toys were less than 99 cents. The coins were great for the weekly visits to the store, Farmer's Market, in Calipatria, California. Thanks to the change, I bought a toy at our shopping day for the *provisiones* (groceries/provisions). Rodo also brought us delicious fruit he had picked from the orchards. The fine, packed fruit was a welcome treat from Rodo's work. Rodo was also one of the last members of the "U.S. Government Bracero Program" in the early sixties.

Rodo, one of my funniest brothers, uses simple nature for the punch lines of his unexpected jokes. His wit is superior, and his sense of humor is impromptu and natural. No matter what age, Rodo dances, jumps and laughs at the simplest of things, creating a spirited and welcoming ambience around him. Many of us think he is fortunate to have nine children and many grandchildren and new great-grandchildren.

Rodo was followed by María del Refugio, born on Uncle Sam's birthday in 1939. No one in our Mexican village knew then that this was Uncle Sam's birthday; otherwise, she might have been named "America" for the hope and dreams of the "American dream." My sister, Cuca, short for María del Refugio, entered the convent of the order of the *Sagrada Familia* (Holy Family) at a young age and was a full-fledged nun by the time I turned five. She lived in many indigenous towns far from our village but within the State of Michoacan. On one occasion, she was sent to Managua, Nicaragua for a few years.

My warmhearted childhood memories of my sister, the nun, are from our various visits to her assignments in the small indigenous villages of Michoacán. Her long, dark-blue habit and the long strand of black rosary beads hanging from her waist made her seem much taller than she really was.

As a child, I wondered why she never changed into different and more colorful clothes, and always wore the same habit. Besides her clothes, her sleeping quarters provoked much curiosity. I always wondered what was behind the fancy, white-pleated curtains in the quarters of the religious order of the Holy Family. Cuca has perhaps received the largest number of our American gifts during the past forty years. Cuca was showered with highly-regarded

American-made gifts during each of our yearly trips to México to visit our grandmother, aunts and uncles. The gifts ranged from fancy boxed chocolates to Sears underwear. It was the underwear about which she bragged the most. At her convent, the sisters quickly learned of the American gifts that were brought for Cuca. These gifts made her feel special. "You see, no one else has 'American' made underwear in the convent," she would tell us with much gusto. In turn, we would burst into laughter. To this day, it would be somewhat unexpected to arrive in México without a "little something" for her or my father.

The always-robust and jolly third brother, Alfonso, was born in July of 1941. At a young age, all our relatives recognized his joyous and jokester personality. His good nature has become his trademark. Not a moment in his presence goes by without the sound of laughter from a joke, poking fun at someone else in the family and rarely at himself. His jokes are strategically planned. His charismatic personality brings laughter to those around him.

He wholeheartedly believes that he has inherited the prettiest feet of us all and is proud to show off their smooth white skin. He reminds us that he is also is the only brother with a full head of hair. As he watches his favorite baseball game, he will make sure to show-off his well proportioned feet. His feet make him proud because much of the rest of the skin on his arms and face is rough, battered by the sun and outdoor life at the feedlot. Alfonso is the only brother whose nickname, "Tite," (no specific meaning) is well-known throughout our small village. As he grew older and heavier, his friends added "La Torta" to the list of acceptable names. Alfonso's rosy-red cheeks and his contagious laughter go well with his nicknames.

A deep compassion for people is a constant value for Alfonso. Al, as his friends in the United States refer to him, is always ready for a party, so much so that he mastered the art of cooking *carnitas* (fried pork meat and a finger-licking and popular dish in Michoacán). *El Chef Torta* has perfected his skills, making him a popular invitee to family gatherings. His younger year's zeal for dancing tango *zapateado* (Mexican traditional dancing by stomping the feet in time with the drum beats and trumpet sounds) with traditional Mexican music has not changed one bit. Our mother had two favorite stories of Alfonso. She always reminded us of the story of his insistent refusal to pray the rosary and the story of him dancing in the middle of a crowd with his pants all torn around the buttocks. Both stories continue today to revive enjoyable memories of our past.

The familiar and popular true story of the devil (or some other force) dragging him from the Mexican adobe home in the fifties is told over and over again. If a person does not believe in evil, he or she will after Alfonso tells his version and reconstruction of this surreal event.

My soft-spoken mother warmly reminded us of the time Alfonso was dragged toward the wooden door in the middle of the night. Alfonso explains in colorful words the story as my mother pulled him back into bed during this horrifying experience. The following morning, my brother had his face marked by what appeared to be sharp fingernail scratches all over his face. This frightening night for Alfonso and my mother proved to be the last time he would defy my mother's orders to pray the rosary with the rest of the family. Mother frequently used this story to remind us of the lessons learned from Alfonso's dispassion for the rosary until this incident. From then on, praying together was never questioned again.

Luis was born in 1944. The soft-spoken brother with a sharp talent for business successfully bridged two cultures before anyone else in the family. His business sense began back in our small village in La Yerbabuena, México. Luis was responsible for the management and operation of the small pantry of goods sold to the villagers. The small store carried large tin containers of lard and sugar. Huge burlap sacks filled with other supplies were always stacked against the walls of our adobe home.

Luis always wore an old storekeeper's heavy apron with many old and new stains of petroleum oil and lard. His shoes also showed signs of a store keeper. He allowed me enough freedom to sneak into the tiny storeroom to eat large chunks of hardened chocolate, sold to families to mix with water or milk for a delicious drink. Everyone rich and poor bought the chunks of chocolate. The poor people used water for the chocolate, and the financially stable families made theirs with milk. My mother reminded us that some of our foods were "*como agua para chocolate.*" I am sure Luis knew who was taking what from his well-organized, humble family business.

Luis is my brother who, in the early 60's, could move to the newest dance-craze, the "Twist" like no other. His sense of humor was more silly than funny. He teased us by dancing the lively "Twist" and suddenly freezing like a statue, pointing his finger at us so that we could again move into the quick-moving Twist. Today, because of his quiet and serious nature, it is difficult to imagine that he was involved in any past shenanigans.

In the late sixties, there was a time of great sadness in our family. The painful news from the Army that Luis had been injured in Vietnam, thousands of miles away, petrified the family, and more so my mother. This was one of the first times that the mortification of such news caused many tears to flow from my mother's pretty eyes. Furthermore, the family was informed that Luis would remain in Okinawa during the long and painful recuperation period. My mother's burden was heavy, and her pain was noticeable.

Luis has an inspiring and heartwarming story that he rarely tells. According to Luis, his life was saved by a *guayaba* (guava) tree he found in the lush jungle of Vietnam. At the time, Luis, the point man for a recognizance unit, came across the tree full of *guayaba* fruit. He asked the second soldier in line to lead while he examined the delicious familiar fruit. No one else in the unit seemed to recognize the delectable *guayabas*. The *guayaba* tree reminded him of our grandfather Antonio's *guayaba* orchard. As his unit continued through the thick foliage, Luis was left behind. Not more than a few minutes later, the point man was shot by a sniper. The short delay with the guayaba tree probably saved Luis from the fatal shot. My mother was always sharing this story, as it made her feel that her *defunto* (deceased) father had somehow played a role in saving Luis through the *guayaba* tree. This rarely-voiced story of his Vietnam experience (1968-1969) is a good indicator of the deep humility and personalized pain that only his heart and soul know. Only recently, Luis began sharing a little more about this difficult time within our family structure and throughout the United States.

Upon his return from the military service, Luis brought tape-playing machines to replace the traditional record player. He spent hours with the skinny and shiny tape meandering from one reel to the other on the face of the boxy equipment. While we were learning the more sophisticated English words, Luis was introducing us to the new rock sounds, including music from the Beatles and the Monkeys. Of course, he did not want us to mess with his delicate yet fancy tape player machines.

On Mother's Day 1974, while I was in my third year at Whittier College, the small home we had in Niland burned down. All but a few belongings were destroyed. Besides my college classmates collecting a whopping three hundred dollars for my family, it was Luis who encouraged my parents to find immediate solutions to the dilemma. A brand-new, single house trailer was purchased, thanks to the help that Luis provided my non-English speaking parents. My parents were pleased to have a quick resolution to the unfortunate turn of events with the destructive fire.

The eighth child, Hector, was born in 1947, following a difficult time for my mother. Nevertheless, Hector became important to the family structure because he was neither the oldest nor the youngest. He interacted wisely with the older siblings while trying to maintain authority over the younger sisters. His skillful application of psychology on the younger sisters usually kept him safe from disciplinary consequences.

Hector probably is the best impromptu story-teller of the entire family. He is skillful at adding his own spice to the stories, turning them into funny events and jokes at family gatherings. Rather than dressing up to play the different characters in his stories, Hector agilely moves his arms and legs to compliment his facial expressions while everyone is laughing at his dramatics. With his natural skills, Hector would be a true champion at Toastmasters.

As a young child, his abilities with the slingshot were refined, hitting the planned targets with ease. He was also swift at aiming and hitting his bird and rabbit targets. Once he hit my sister, Blanca, with a small rock. The perfect aim below the young knee prompted a great deal of commotion from my mother. An unexpected, gushing flow of red blood poured from her injury.

Everyone knew that Hector had been seriously reprimanded for his sharp target skills. The internal sibling rivalry never stopped until we all moved away from our parents' home. Our sibling rivalry was no different than what exists in most normal and content families.

When we lived in México, I remember Hector always trying to hit some type of target with this homemade sling shot. To this day, every September he goes hunting for the same dove in order to have the tasty green tomatillos sauce and *guilota* (white-winged dove) dish served with fresh-made and steamy corn tortillas.

Growing up, Hector's quips and quotes attached to his non-verbal messages, brought life to our long, daily rosaries. Many of these rosaries will probably never count toward our efforts to go to heaven, since he frequently provoked us behind my mother's back. Hector orchestrated the silent symphony of non-verbal comedy, instigating our unexpected laughter, followed by reprimands from our mother for disturbing the sacred rosary.

As a child, Hector loved to play with tin trucks, pretending he was the driver. He would make motor sounds with his mouth as he guided the hot red painted toy trucks up and down the play slopes of mud. His hands were filthy from his hand-made mud hills. My sister Blanca and I on occasion were allowed to join him with our own red and blue tin trucks.

In 1948, only eleven months after Hector's birth, Silvino was born.

At six months, baby Silvino died of some sort of unidentified infection. Regretfully, he died in my mother's arms on route to see the doctor. The child was buried without much fanfare by my grandparents. He was always remembered by my mother until her final living moments. For many years my mother deeply regretted not knowing where her baby was buried. This matter never left my mother, as it was a heart felt loss of her baby boy named after our father.

The dearest of my sisters was born in January 1951 and was named after the famous movie star of México, Blanca Estella Pavon. Estelle was the preferred name in elementary and high school. People in those days could not understand the word "Blanca" as a proper name. Blanca, like the wings of bamboo, was my constant protector and support system as a young child and during my high school years. She was the defender of my mischief in front of the family. She stood up for me during squabbles over nothing. She often sacrificed her few dollars to see me at the high school prom and involved in school events.

Blanca constantly and unselfishly paved the road for my creative *travesuras* (mischief) that were successfully blended into the everyday life of the family. She allowed and tolerated my teasing her for her freckled face as a teenager when I called her *cara de huevo de curuca* (turkey egg face). Her freckles prominently stood out against her very light skin.

One of the most memorable childhood experiences that Blanca

and I shared took place when she was about six years old and I was nearly five years of age. My mother allowed us to take the *burro* (donkey) with the large empty *cántaros* (pottery jugs) to refill them with fresh spring water. We were so small that the process of getting on the burro was a laborious one. We guided the animal next to a large, volcanic rock by the corral. The large, porous rock was our only way of escalating to the top layers of the rough burlap on the spine of the long-eared animal. The *cántaros* rested against the edges of the burlap. The soft belly of the burro provided the *cántaros* enough cushion for a tranquil ride to the watering hole.

Blanca and I were thrilled that our mother allowed us to venture into the adult world of household chores. We met up with an untamed burro as we rode toward the spring water hole. Our slow-moving and domesticated donkey became restless and aggravated as the other burro tried to intimidate and bully him to no end. It was clear to us that what would follow would turn into a donkey brawl.

In a sudden and unexpected reaction, both burros became agitated, trying to bite at each other. Both donkeys tried to reach each other's long and hairy necks. The big teeth of both animals were visible to us as we screamed for help and bawled for immediate salvation. Both donkeys became loud and aggressive as they kicked up their hind legs and farted at the same time. Normally, the farting of the *burros* was funny, but we were not laughing. Instead, my sister and I were terrified. Adults in our village knew very well that when sounds came from both ends of certain animals, there was cause for concern, particularly with their horses, donkeys and mules. Our kind neighbors immediately came out to the cobblestone path to help us and provided a welcome rescue. We were assisted off the spirited donkey. The neighbors must have noticed how frightened we were as they called out for my mother and others. Immediately, gave us a mixture of salt and uncooked green leaves. Supposedly, chewing on the leaves calmed our nerves and fears. My mother was extremely nervous about the entire incident involving the donkey. This was the first and last time Blanca and I rode a donkey together.

During the rough and tough teenage years, my sister conspired with me to ensure that our visits to the Pico Rivera, California libraries were also visits to meet with my favorite friends (boys). The escape to meet the boys at the City library was orchestrated with the promise to return home at the expected and exact time. There was no deviation from that! Not following the rules led to some deserved punishment. I made sure to cover up the social nature of the library visits by checking out additional books of science and history to carry home. The books always ended up on the kitchen table to support the academic efforts of the night.

Blanca's tolerance for life's challenges appeared early, as she faced my ongoing demands for doing things so differently. She is probably the luckiest of the siblings in many respects. The one magical touch that Blanca possesses is that she is a magnet to children of all ages. Children have followed her like the "Pied

Piper." No matter what time of the day or night you arrive at her home, the sounds and sights of children were always present. All the grown children remember the joyful pizza parties and festive ice cream socials held for no special reason at Blanca's house. Celebrations were common every weekend at her house and every child's birthday was a real bash.

During my mother's last pregnancy, my father was in the United States working as a *Bracero* (laborer for Mexican worker program) in Santa María, California. As I have been told many times, my father wrote to my mother, expressing his wish to name the soon-to-be-born new baby after him. If the child was a boy, he wanted him named Silvino; and if the child was a girl, she would be named Silvia. It was settled; my name was going to be Silvia.

During delivery, my mother had a difficult time giving birth. Her pain and suffering drove the women of the village, including my sister María Elena, to prayer asking the different saints for a safe delivery. After a lengthy labor, I was finally born.

The soft light of the flickering candles finally welcomed the last of the children born to María de los Ángeles and Silvino Zendejas. I am told that the family was bursting with joy at the arrival of the new baby girl. The eager-to-burn yellow wax candles provided enough light for the village midwife, Maximiana, to work her miracles on the pregnant women of the isolated village. Tiny babies emerged from the big bellies of the Mexican women, while the men anxiously waited, quaffing any worries with delicious homemade tequila and *pulque* (unfermented juice from the heart of the agave cactus). All the babies in this tiny village were born in their homes on hard wooden beds or *petates* (woven weed mats). The fresh mountain air welcomed all new babies to the Mexican village.

I was born in a simple *adobe* (mud and hay bricks baked under the sun) home in México. My mother told me that mine was a difficult delivery for her. At the time of my birth, my father was working in the United States of America in the town of Santa María, which is north of Santa Barbara, California. My mother's companions during her final labor and delivery included my older brothers and sisters.

I was born on the Patron Saint Day of Our Lady of Esperanza, a much-celebrated day in the bustling town of Jacona, Michoacán. Appropriately since such pain and suffering passed without major incident, I was christened María Esperanza in honor of the patron Saint, Esperanza. In our village, all the females were named María, followed by another Christian name. This was no exception to the girls born to our parents. My sister indicates that the name of Silvia was purposely dropped since so much prayer was offered to the Virgin of Esperanza, and the Saint complied with this humble request. In English, Esperanza means hope. Esperanza is the hope that the people of poverty rely and depend on. The name is a noble one, respected by those that have little and hope for more.

By the time I was an energetic toddler, I was fortunate to have several sets of siblings old enough to be my parents. The love and guidance I received from my brothers, sisters and mother instilled key values in me. Like many immigrants of the past and present, my father, while away in the United States, sent money to México to support the large and growing family.

I was extremely lucky to have lived and worked with such a dynamic group of siblings and friends, all of whom added a unique wealth of information, expertise, love and support. I had all I needed from my family to succeed in life. My large family had all the personalities of a well-written documentary. I was truly blessed to have had such a world-class stage on which to perform my simple growing-up routines without fear of failure. My multigenerational family was always there during my early and impressionable years.

I developed a strong sense of curiosity at an early age. I attributed much of my curiosity to growing up with friendly animals and to growing up in the country with a large family. The chickens, donkeys, cows, horses, dogs and critters added much color to my childhood. The distant coyotes howling under the moonlit skies always brought a sense of apprehension, forcing me to seek the warmth of my mother or to lie next to one of my funny brothers.

The chickens and the birds of our native México inspired much of my present love for feathered friends. I was fascinated mostly by the eggs that magically appeared under the fluffy feathers of the fowl. For some unknown purpose, birds and their eggs became important to me. Perhaps one reason is the multi-use of the egg. Growing up, I remember using eggs to sew my father's and brothers' old and torn socks. My mother taught me how to stick the largest egg we could find into the torn sock. Once the un-raveling part of the sock was reached, the white of the egg shell could be seen. The needle and thread were used to sew the loose fibers of the socks together. The socks were soon repaired, thanks to the egg. As teenagers, our only pair of stockings was also sewn in this manner.

Shortly before we immigrated to the United States, I enrolled in the Catholic school in La Yerbabuena. It was the only school in our village. The nuns managed the school. Since my mother provided strong support for the school, she sent me to school with goodies to sell to other children to help raise money for the nuns. After school, I carried a tray of *bolitas de leche* (small balls of burnt milk) that my mother made for me to sell. I was about five years old and was learning the marketing skills of selling. My mother spent many hours mixing fresh cow's milk and sugar until it formed a bronze-glazed and sticky substance. While the mixture was hot, my mother rolled the substance into small balls, smaller than golf balls. I sold the brown candies after school, and sometimes gave them away to my friends that did not have the money to purchase them. I sold the candied milk for *un centavo* (one cent). My mother was highly regarded and respected by the nuns for raising money for the Catholic school with her popular milk candies.

During my first years in the United States, we enrolled in Niland Elementary School, in the Imperial Valley. At first, I did not have many friends, due to the fact that I did not speak English; this changed in later grades as my English improved. Besides not knowing the language during my first years in elementary school, I was very different since I had very light blond hair. The lack

of English and my looking different prompted certain students to pinch my arms. For a long period of time, the pinch marks remained as subtle reminders of my hesitation toward strangers. This unfortunate experience brought me closer to my parents and siblings. By the time I was in third grade, the pinching stopped. My limited language abilities to fend for myself and my hair turning dark created a smoother transition into the new culture.

Niland School, now the Grace Smith Elementary School, was completely diverse in the early sixties. My classes were made up of students from a variety of ethnic and cultural backgrounds. Our school had Chinese, Filipino, Mexican and Anglo students. Our teachers were all Anglo. The only employees who spoke Spanish were the cafeteria workers, bus drivers and custodians. I became good friends with the custodian, cafeteria workers and our bus driver, Rocky.

In upper elementary school grades, I worked in the cafeteria with the ladies helping serve lunch for the other students. With our family's anemic budget, this was a great benefit for our parents, since lunch was free for the student workers. I clearly remember one of the cafeteria workers asking me to marry her son once I was old enough to marry. I guess she must have thought I was a nice girl in the elementary school.

At school, I dedicated most of my free time to playing sports with the boys. At home, instead of playing with jacks or Barbie dolls, I enjoyed the company of the many birds that grazed in the open fields near the feedlot by our home. I loved to watch them build their nests, lay their eggs, and hatch their babies. I kept track of the young chicks' first flights. There were hundreds of nests in the trees that shaded the corrals and in the tall grasses around the reservoir. Their activities mesmerized me, and for a time I spoke of nothing else. One day, I even gathered twenty of the tiny bird eggs in an attempt to make a fried egg breakfast for my father.

During the summer months, I continued to play with birds and their eggs. A feedlot in the Imperial Valley was a perfect place for birds and nests. For several summers, I tried frying birds' eggs on the hot pavement of the 120 degree weather. I had heard that eggs could be fried on the Imperial Valley paved roads. Birds' eggs did fry on the pavement, but not as quickly as they would in hot lard.

My special hobby became evident in grade school, as I often took birds' eggs to science class for "show and tell" and sometimes just for fun. Many were babies that had fallen from the nest, and I hand-fed them in hopes that they survived. I took the babies and sometimes their mothers to school along with a variety of nests, fresh and old. On many such occasions, the birds did not survive

the school bus ride or their new schoolhouse living conditions.
My classmates took notice that the birds often died in my
care and soon began to tease me. I was not upset by the nickname, "Bird Killer." I did not like it, but knew it was not true. I
loved birds, and it was a natural consequence that some died.
Many of them were just tiny baby birds. I always rationalized their
deaths as the fault of teachers who did not allow me to feed the
hungry feathered creatures during class.

For several years during elementary school, my brothers were not
happy with one of my friends. Her name was Thelma Lewis. She
was my classmate. Thelma's family had come to the Imperial
Valley from Oklahoma. She had pretty red hair and many freckles
on her white face and arms. She also lived out in the country, next
to the new geothermal plant several miles to the west of our
country home near the Salton Sea. Thelma's father worked at the
geothermal plant.

Thelma was notorious for telephoning our house very early in the
morning long before the school bus arrived. She was like an alarm
clock for all of us. Her calls became a nuisance to my family since
we were not accustomed to having a phone, let alone having it ring
loudly in the very early mornings. My brothers pleaded and
insisted that I tell her not to bother us so early. I did not have
the heart to tell Thelma not to call the house. She wanted to know
what I was going to wear on the given day. Secondly, Thelma
wanted me to make sure I saved her a seat on the bus. When the
telephone rang, my brothers and sister would mimic Thelma with

some funny sort of muffled and nasal sounds, and then they would laugh out loud before moving on to getting ready for school. I don't think Thelma ever knew of this silly matter happening at our home. Once we all got on the bus, nobody said anything about the phone calls from Thelma. My brothers went to the back of the bus where all the high school bus students would sit. I would sit in the front of the bus with Thelma. Everyone tended to their own business on the school bus. To this day, I can almost hear the sounds coming from my brothers mimicking, "Thellllmmma!"

By seventh grade, my friends had heard my family calling me Espy, short for Esperanza. Espy sounds like the two letters "S" and "P," which, as fate had it, were the initials of the Southern Pacific rail line. Instead of being called a tomboy, I was nicknamed after the powerful "SP" engines that rolled into Niland on a daily basis — huge, shiny bolts of steel pulling hundreds of box cars through the California desert. My classmates, many of them sons and daughters of railroad workers, thought that calling me SP, Southern Pacific, aptly reflected my competitive nature. The nicknames came and went as I grew and changed, but each one still brings back special memories of significant times in my life. At El Rancho High School, the superintendent referred to me as "Queenie," after I became the first Sixteenth of September Queen for Pico Rivera, California.

By the time I was in eighth grade, five of my brothers and sisters had left the comfort of our home to form and start their own families. To date, our family includes a total of thirty-six grandchildren, sixty-five great-grandchildren and three great-great-grandchildren.

My brothers and sisters probably remember me as the "*gordita del perro*," (the dog's biscuit) as mother would refer to the youngest of her children. All of my family recalls the crochet hats that mother made me for my birthdays. As I grew older, I hated to wear the droopy and silly crochet hat but never dared say much since my mother had done so many other things for me on these special days. As a matter of fact, I instigated many of the events on my saint's day, September 8th. Often, we prepared special foods to celebrate "la gordita del perro's" birthday.

On my ninth birthday, I convinced my mother to allow me to wear my pretty white post-communion dress, which she had purchased in the United States. My father drove my mother, Hector, Blanca and I to Mexicali for the normal weekend trip. During our Mexicali visits, my father would get his conservative-style haircut of the sixties, while my mother shopped around and attended mass in Baja California's capitol city.

After mass in the cathedral, politely, I scurried my mother and siblings into a photography shop. My intentions were clear; the photographer would take my picture and record the special moment. These photography shops were numerous on border towns. This was the first time that I would have a professional picture taken on my very own birthday. The color picture of my birthday would be just like the ones displayed in the large glass windows. The only professional photograph we had ever taken together was for our passports and immigration documents.

Like a great psychologist, the photographer read our non-verbal thoughts and immediately walked us into his lighted studio with a black curtain of sorts hanging from the ceiling. I remember telling the man that it was my birthday, at which time he immediately realized that I was the only interested party. From one of the corners, he pulled a wooden *pastel* (cake) finely decorated with dainty pastel painted flowers. It was a beautiful cake of numerous layers with fake decorated icing. The cake looked real!

Next, I was graciously arranged by the big *pastel* (cake) as if I was part royalty. The photographer politely placed a knife in my right hand while he located my left hand softly touching the edge of the large platter holding the beautiful fake *pastel*. I held my breath as the bright lights and the additional flashing of lights glared in our faces. Humbleness was nowhere to be found; instead, I felt like María Felix, the famous Mexican movie star, performing on stage.

Blanca and Hector just waited for this boring and useless time to quickly come to an end. It was obvious that they were just being obedient in front of our mother. Unbeknownst to them, my mother, in her style and surprising approach, ordered Hector and Blanca to stand next to me for another setting with the three of us. We were the youngest of her off-spring, and no one would argue with her proud intentions to show off her handsome children in a color photograph. My mother's eyes were on every detail during the unexpected photo shoot. Both Hector and Blanca's facial expressions changed as if a pail of iced water had been tossed at them. They did not want to take the picture since they had not prepared their wardrobe. They were not happy people, but their brief discontent had nowhere to go. My mother's orders were always final. Hector slowly shuffled his way to the spot where he was to stand. Blanca stared at me as if I were the person responsible for this unexpected moment.

The photographer immediately organized us for the photo, from the tallest to the shortest. The photograph shop owner sensed the discomfort in my brother's and sister's body language, in their eyes and in their unenthusiastic smiles. He moved rather quickly to accommodate the camera-shy uneasiness. Within seconds, he snuck under a heavy black blanket behind the boxy camera. Another bright and bold flash spotlighted the three youngest children of Silvino and María Zendejas. In the meantime, in the same flash speed, Hector and Blanca left me standing in the spot as if I had some type of contagious disease. By the time I caught on, my mother smiled with relief and was glad that she had accomplished her unsuspected mission.

This infamous family picture brings many fond memories of the patience and dedication of eight siblings in raising the youngest of the family during a time of welcomed change for all of us. The cover picture is the outcome of a proud mother watching her three youngest together in a classic moment.

Life has a way of providing heartfelt memories that keep one's spirit alive. The experiences of growing up with solid family values, support and a strong faith have provided me with a meaningful purpose in life. Today, I firmly believe that I am a woman of two souls, two languages, and an endless amount of energy, much indebted to the encouragement, expectation and love from an entire family made up of sisters, brothers, parents, grand-parents, uncles and aunts. The family has done well with the many lessons we have learned together. I am certain that through our faith, we can share these lessons with the generations that follow.

Fiesta

Some of the happiest moments, filled with laughter, music and great *antojitos* (snacks), were during the fiestas of our patriotic and religious Mexican village. Many villages, including our own isolated home, have a patron saint who serves as the exclusive guardian of the people, the crops, the homes, and the animals. In La Yerbabuena, Michoacán, the *Virgen de Guadalupe* looked over us from a large painting that hung against the wall facing the church pews. Several smaller statues of the *Virgen* also adorned the adobe church, and graced every home altar. I remember that in some homes, the altars for her were elaborate. During certain yearly times, the altars were adorned with additional colorful *papel de China* (tissue paper) for the festivities to honor the patron saint of our village.

The entire country of México commemorates the *Virgen de Guadalupe's* birthday on December 12, but in La Yerbabuena she is also honored on January 11 and 12, a time when the men and women who work in the California fields return home for the winter and during the season where less harvesting occurs. The huge fiesta for the Virgin was held to thank her for the many blessings she had granted during the year. These happy days often provided an opportunity for the villagers to schedule other special events, such as marriages, baptisms, first communions, and confirmations. Everyone — from the children to the elders — always had special traditions to look forward to during these fiestas, including me.

No one ever forgets the start of the fiesta, as it symbolizes the powerful influence of the Virgin and *Santos* in everything we did in the village. Between midnight's moon and the first light of dawn on January 11, twenty musicians played the traditional *mañanitas* (Mexican birthday song) to herald the celebration. Closure to the fiesta was signaled by the band playing the emotional farewell to the Virgin with the *Golondrinas* (song of the swallows). At the center of the plaza was the large adobe church where the band gathered at the start and end of the fiestas.

In the church, women waited while the men ushered the musicians from one end of the village into the church. The sounds of gun powder exploding in the air signaled the glorious time of celebration and honor for the *Virgen de Guadalupe.* The gun powder slightly tinted the cool air with a burnt smell of fireworks. Without any electricity or phones in the village as distractions, the sounds and different odors captivated everyone's focused festive attention.

The distant howling coyotes chimed in with the beating of the drums and the loud, old trumpets playing in the church, before any of the village roosters began their morning routine. As the music swelled inside the adobe church, swallows swooped near the towering ceiling of the mission-style building, as if dancing in gusto for the saints standing firmly at the base of the altar. The smell of church incense was also a symbol of the special occasion. The rhythm of the drums and trumpets made the poor peoples' hearts beat with pride, including my family's and mine. Inside my body, it was as if I had a drum playing, as the noise penetrated through my heart, causing strong vibrations. These sounds, unbeknownst to me at the time, would forever be a part of my culture.

For most of the families, the fiesta meant new fabric to be bought and sewn into simple clothes for everyone. The young women, in particular, could not wait to see what everyone else was wearing to compare the best-dressed. Often, the women chose colorful fabrics and traditional textiles to adorn their new fiesta dresses. Fashion in our village was associated with color. There was very little effort from the grown-ups to match colors or pattern combinations during my early years in our village. Being fashion-able during these times did not include matching tops and bot-toms, shirts, ties or other accessories. Unless there were women mourning loved ones, the colorful dresses for women and the bright shirts for men were well-suited for the special event. The excitement of the fiesta lingered in the air long before the celebration began.

My favorite part of the fiesta was the huge wooden merry-go-round powered by human muscle. The merry-go-round, called the *Ola* or Wave, was about twice the circumference of a huge parachute. Men, women, and children climbed up a portable and squeaky wooden staircase to sit on the stationary benches along the loosely arranged planks of the outer ring.

As soon as everyone was onboard, workers removed the portable stairs, and then four to six men began to turn the large circular wheel, pushing with their hands on thick round handles that stuck out of the sides of the wooden planks. As the merry-go-round picked up speed, the men pushing the ride had to hold on for dear life. The *Ola* not only turned in dizzy circles but also rose off the ground, lifting the men into the air. The men pushing and being lifted into the air amazed those onboard and those looking from the ground waiting to be next. Everyone laughed and cheered at the colorful and dizzy-like motions of the merry-go-round.

The women screamed, as the *Ola* lifted on one of its sides, as if it were Marilyn Monroe's dress in the famous picture of her skirt caught by the wind. The muscle men looked confident surfing the in the merry-go-ground wind in the circus-like atmosphere. They held onto their hats as the *Ola* swung up, up and down, down and around. A manual power plant provided the meager lighting that decorated the center of this entertaining equipment.

La Yerbabuena had no electricity. Candles provided light for night sewing, cooking and other expected tasks. During the days of the fiesta, our village sparkled like a basket full of diamonds. Portable generators were brought to power light bulbs for the game areas.

Lotería (lottery), a game similar to American bingo played with pictures, instead of letters and numbers and corn and beans to mark the pictures, was a popular stop for all the fiesta attendees. The area for *lotería* was set up in a large, rectangular area outlined with tiny round lights tied from pole to pole. Contestants paid the *cinco centavos* (five cents) to sit on hard benches made from wooden planks. Wooden planks also served as long tables where the playing cards waited for the kernels of corn. I could not see above the shoulders of those sitting on the planks frantically calling out "*Buena!*" (Good one!).

My small frame and short stature did not allow me to poke through the crowd. I barely could see between the big sombreros worn by the men playing *lotería*. The players who thought they had a winning combination would yell so that the *lotería* game could be stopped for a moment while the winning cards were reviewed again. The colorful clothing created an unforgettable range of seated rear ends of varying sizes tightly squeezed together on the wooden planks. The tapestry of colorful butts created the potential for an award-winning photo-graph for *National Geographic*, forming an eye-catching view for a child.

These games were too fast for children to participate, so many of us watched from nearby to see who won the pre-announced household prizes. The so-called host called off the picture of the next card in the deck he had shuffled in front of the eyes of the optimistic players. The players placed corn kernels or pinto beans on the pictures to mark their entrées.

A cheerful male voice amplified by a generator-operated microphone could be heard all over the village, hollering clues for each picture he drew from a deck of cards before announcing the full card. The man gave a description for each picture card, such as, "*La campana* (the bell): she calls you to church." He followed by soundly repeating "*la campana*." I do not remember any women helping behind the wooden planks. This was surely a male-dominated event.

People playing the game who had a picture of a bell on their cards added a kernel of yellow or blue corn or a pinto bean to the appropriate square. When a player had enough pictures covered to win the game, he or she yelled out "*Buena!*" As in bingo, the picture card was reviewed by game monitors to make sure it was marked correctly. The winner usually won porcelain cups or small buckets made of galvanized tin.

The aromas of the fiesta were fresh and sweet. Women took their piles of wood along with three volcanic rocks the size of soccer balls and copper pots to get their *antojitos* (goodies) ready to serve. The three rocks formed a base for the pot, and between the rocks, pieces of wood burned for the women to cook, while smoke lingered in the festive air. A high stack of fragile, large fried tortillas surfaced like church steeples out of woven baskets. The fried tortillas were crushed into boiling brown sugar and served piping hot on pieces of brown, butcher-type paper. The hot *buñuelos* (fritters) were delicious with hot, sweet *atole* (liquid corn meal).

The homemade goods were often sold by women sitting on short wooden stools spreading apart their skirted legs, while their long dresses and aprons formed folds of clothing practically over the fire. The women frying *buñuelos* used shiny copper pots for boiling small amount of water and pieces of hardened brown sugar. After the ingredients melted in front of the savoring onlookers, the women took two or three flour tortilla discs and broke them into the copper kettle while quickly stirring with a wooden spoon. The scent of burnt sugar and flour tortillas rose in flares and puffs of open-market smoke signals, bringing more people to the cooking area. The refried tortillas were tossed into sweet and gummy "buñuelos."

The colors of the fiesta were also found on the cobble-stone plaza as many indigenous vendors came down from the surrounding mountains, bringing their home-grown goods for sale. The sharp red, white, orange and greens of flowers, fruits and vegetables were spread on hand-woven blankets for people to walk by and select for purchase. The fruits and vegetables, gently organized in piles of eight or four, enticed shoppers with their colors. The fresh smell of cilantro and onion was evident as we walked between the colorful blankets displaying the home-grown produce. I would

refer to these products as "blanket produce." We were told
that some of the baked bread was also covered with blankets and
bed sheets for the leavening and before it was sold out on the
open-air farmer's market. As a child, this was not encouraging.

On another stand, huge glass containers resembling barrels sat in
rows of six or seven. Each of the containers had a sweet water
mixture with a special flavor creating a special color. The most
popular drinks of tamarind, *jamaica, orchata, límon* and *piña*
flavors were served in recently baked pottery cups. Besides the
brown, red, white, green and yellow colors, the adults and children
marketing these drinks included floating pieces of the fruit in the
large glass jars. The merchant in charge of the outdoor stand
removed the tin top off the glass jar and with a long ladle, poured a
glass full of delicious, mouth-watering flavor for the fiesta attendee
to savor.

Besides the drinks and food, the smell of cooked *agave* fermented
and poured in bottles of tequila danced mischievously throughout
the fiesta. The smell of tequila is a sweet smell that cannot be
confused with another; it was and still is the smell of happiness
and sadness. During the happy fiestas, the smell of fermented
drinks could be detected on many of the men and a few unsus-
pecting women. During funerals it is also prevalent among men
mourning the lost and departed soul to drink their sorrows away
with tequila. At the fiesta, the tequila bottles were often found
empty, waiting for someone else to pick up and refill them at the
tiny mom and pop store. The women often saved the tequila

bottles for a later use in the kitchen or as inexpensive candle holders.

At midnight, everyone gathered in the plaza center of the village to watch the fireworks. Although the complicated *castillo* (firework structure) Eiffel Tower-type structure made of dried bamboo and gunpowder was lit with a single match and burned in just a few minutes, the pyrotechnics it created delighted the people and sparked much interest in all of us. This burning of the bamboo *castillo* event was the evening's finale. A band played while the burning shoots of bamboo exploded into colorful rays of brilliant sparks. While the grownups clapped and cheered for the stunning display, the children chased the sparks in hopes of getting burns on their clothes as evidence of their bravery.

When the spectacle ended, families walked home under the moonlight. A few people carried candles on cloudy nights, and the flickering lights danced off the cobblestones as the sleepy villagers returned to their adobe homes. With the musicians gone and the electric generators silenced, a beautiful quiet descended on the mountain village. Only the hoot of an owl or the howl of a coyote in the distance broke the enviable spell. On full moon nights, candles were not necessary. The moon provided much of the silvery light reflecting off the large cactus leaves, creating rustic shadows against the whitewash adobe homes.

In our village, many children were born during the quiet of autumn. The fiesta had an overwhelming effect on families in many different and significant ways. Many of the men returned to México to celebrate the fiesta with other family members.

In my family, we laugh at the successes of the fiestas as noted by

our birthdates. In fact, most of my siblings were born after July and before November. I was born in September, 1952. The January 1952 fiesta must have been a memorable one for my parents. It is evident that the happiness of both of my parents was shared with all of their children. The happiness is visible in the eyes of every son and daughter.

When we arrived in the United States, we reminisced about the fiesta on every January 12 with stories of the past fiestas. Life changed for us in so many unexpected ways. We were fortunate that our father had the wisdom to bring us to the country, where the memories of our village seem so close, especially at night under the stars. For some reason, I always thought that the stars had followed us and had parked themselves overhead to keep us company. The donkeys, pigs, chickens, roosters and coyotes were replaced by loud, romantic frogs, sleepy, fluffy owls, noisy birds, fat cattle and occasional crop dusters in the early hours of dawn. The country and rural surroundings of California held together strings of the heart, connecting us from our past to the present, allowing a tender bridging of cultures, languages and friends.

My mother made sure that we continued to observe certain traditional holidays, such as Good Friday, Palm Sunday, Easter and Christmas with special prayers and other spiritual practices.

As children, our favorite celebration was *el día de los Tres Reyes Magos* (Wise Men). This was our gift-receiving day. Every January 5th our tattered shoes were located near the door so that the *Tres Reyes Magos* could find them and leave their goods behind. This was extremely important to the children in our village. For a few years in the United States, we continued leaving our shoes by the door. Later, this special day seemed to be consumed by the colorful, jolly, bearded and *panzón* (large-bellied) man.

Although we did not spend much time celebrating *Cinco de Mayo* (a celebration honoring a historical victory against the French soldiers), we did pay much attention to the Mexican Independence Day. However, of all days of honor and celebration, the day reserved for *Nuestra Señora de Guadalupe* (Our Lady of Guadalupe) was the most important day of the year. Our religious observances were important in helping us retain our Mexican culture, while we assimilated to the rituals of our new country.

Singing songs was my mother's favorite way of honoring the *Virgen de Guadalupe*. My mother taught us all of the songs of many generations past to honor the Virgin. She also made sure we prayed the rosary as a family on a daily basis. There was no deviation from this expectation. She always reminded us that singing was the same as praying and that praying always kept the family together. The fiesta song I remember best included the following words:

*Desde el cielo una hermosa mañana, desde el
cielo una hermosa mañana, la Guadalupana, la
Guadalupana, la Guadalupana bajo el Tepeyac
desde el cielo*...(from the sky a beautiful morning,
from the sky a beautiful morning, the Lady Guadalupe,
the Lady Guadalupe...)

Fiestas in our village were times of magic and wonderment.
During these happy times, the poor and the moribund forgot
about the many challenges facing them. The outcome of the
successful corn crop led to the level of celebration for the villagers.
The sounds of the church bells calling the villagers to church as the
wind instruments played for the *Santos* is embedded in the hearts
of the people of La Yerbabuena, Michoacán.

Mom's Cherished Mexican

Cooking

1952–2001

The unforgettable, delicious and lingering aromas in the
kitchen came from the foods that were prepared for the
family by my dear mother. The transformation of herbs,
spices and other natural foods and meats into scrumptious and
tasty dishes was my mother's way of working her daily magic.
The kitchen was the place where the lasting, spicy aromas merged
into family conversations during our gatherings at La Yerbabuena,
Michoacán, México. The family talked about the day's events and
mañana's (tomorrow's) challenges. The entire happy family
looked forward to the warm Mexican meals prepared with love.

Many of the spices, herbs and edible plants were found in the
gardens of the homes in México. In other cases, the edible plants
and vegetables were found in the sounding, mountainous hills.

The traditional *yerba buena, ruda, ojas de límon, ojas de guayaba* (leaves of lemon, leaves of guayaba), *camote* (sweet potato), *nopales* (cactus), *jicama, calabaza* (squash), *tunas* (cactus prickly pear) and *quelite* (a type of collard greens) were always part of the ingredients and additions to weekly menus in our Mexican home. Much of the foods we ate were greatly influenced by the cultures prior to the Spaniards arriving on the shores México. The Aztecs and other indigenous cultures perhaps contributed most to the culture and traditions of our foods.

In the Californian lower desert, my mother worked tirelessly to grow the same spices and plants that she had planted in our Mexican village. Regretfully, the climate and saline ground in the Imperial Valley were not encouraging for the familiar garden plants. My mother worked meticulously with the salty ground, eventually forcing the growth of the herbs she missed so much. In the absence of the fresh herbs, she added dried cumin, garlic and onions to the Mexican foods of enchiladas, tacos, *caldos* (soups) and rice dishes.

In México, the corn, bean and squash *milpas* (corn crops) were tended in special and caring ways. So much so, that churchgoers prayed for the timely rain to shower on the young crops. Without the rain, the *ardillas* (squirrels) dug the dried beans and corn kernels before the young, green stalks poked through the volcanic and rocky soil. The traditional Mexican food staples were most important to our family's "table of plenty." My mother learned to cook beans, squash and corn in one hundred different ways. It was not out of place to find children and aging grandparents eating the mush made of squash and boiled milk. The corn tortillas and beans were never absent from any of the meals either. To this date, corn must be in the culture of our stomachs, since it is a "must-have" during most meals, no matter where we live. You could say that we were fixated with beans, corn and tortillas.

The squash vines that wrapped themselves around the corn stalks and large, porous rocks provided delicious meals for many months after the fall harvest of the corn. My mother made sure those pots of boiling, fresh corn and squash were on the stove during the harvest season. Without electricity, the prepared foods were always hand-harvested from the green hills or neighboring village. Large baskets woven with cow-skin were used to carry the plucked corn from the stock in the hills. Men and women would carry the unusual baskets on their backs through the zigzagging of the mature corn plants. The long, tongue-like leaves of the corn stock caressed the humble people as they gathered the *maiz, frijoles* and small *calabazas* (corn, beans and squash).

The best beans were those that were picked directly from the vines by the families themselves. Each fresh bean harvest created lasting memories to fill the stomachs for the entire year and until the following harvest. The fresh beans were usually served for breakfast, lunch and dinner. It was also customary to have pots on the open hearth over a flame cooking the traditional *frijoles de la olla* (boiled beans with onions and salt). These *frijoles* were "Crock-Pot" style, since they took forever to cook. The tastiest beans were those fried with lard from a recently butchered pig. My mother often stretched the menu by creating crispy tacos with beans cooked over a low mesquite flame.

Inside our adobe kitchen, the clay open hearth was surrounded by another lower layer of mud bricks. This extra "step-like" space was used as one of our humble eating spaces. This was like a breakfast "nook" of sorts. My brothers and sisters sat next to the open hearth, waiting for the hot tortillas and burnt cheese to fill each hungry stomach. The smell of hot, toasty tortillas usually filled the room with corn aromas of warmth and security. The smell of corn in our village kitchen was warmly related to the entire environment of our surroundings. The corn magically transformed the kitchen into a "peaceful" place for gathering. The burnt cheese and frying peppers left a delicious, pungent odor. The spicy odors of cheese and peppers always escaped the kitchen before our nostrils could consume the entire aroma. Overall, our busy kitchen always smelled very good.

High above the reach of all, thin pieces of beef hung in a clothesline fashion for the drying process to mature. Each piece of drying meat had numerous holes as a result of the very thin cuts. The fresh meat was covered in large grains of salt while the dry pieces were darkened and stiffened by the drying process. During the early morning, the sun rays pushed their way through the tiny holes on the meat, creating mini sun rays from one end of the kitchen to the other. Hanging along with the meat were occasional dry plants and herbs. As a child, the imagery of drying meat and

hanging herbs offered me a sense of abundance during daylight
hours. During late evenings, the drying meat was a ghostly
arrangement against the shadows of the cooking fire.

Thanks to the cracks in the roof between the adobe blocks and
the Mexican roof tile, our kitchen had enough fresh air ventilation.
Air came into our kitchen as the delicious odors escaped through
other small openings to the cobblestone path in front of our adobe
home. This was the same for all the homes in our village made
with *tejas* (Mexican clay roof tile) and adobe. Men, women and
children could easily figure out the type of foods being served at
each home by walking next to the cobblestone paths between the
homes.

Inside the kitchen, family members and the scroungy dogs
patiently waited for the food to be served. As my brothers ate,
small morsels of tortilla were tossed into the air and behind them.
I remember the enthusiastic, four-legged friends watching for my
brother Luis or Rodo, waiting for the flying piece of left-over
tortilla or a small, meatless bone. Along with the family, the dogs
also enjoyed the atmosphere of the warm and welcoming kitchen.
The fancy, yet humble odors of our fried foods and corn enticed
every bit of appetite in the kitchen.

On special days of festive traditions, my mother took a live chicken
and in a matter of hours had it converted to the delicious *pollo en
mole* (chicken with a chocolate and peanut sauce). After the
feathers were plucked, the hot water for cleaning was tossed out

onto the cobblestone-packed patio. The chicken was immediately boiled in water, garlic, salt and onion. Every part of the chicken was prepared for the meal. The preparation of a chicken *mole* meal was definitely time-consuming. The special chicken *mole* was a traditional dish at all wedding celebrations.

Some families chopped the head off the chicken for a quicker preparation process, leading up to the fresh, spicy meal. Other families took the neck of the poor, feathered animal and twisted it until the chicken was left without a head. I am assuming that twisting the neck of the animal required a more courageous woman. No matter which way the chickens were prepared, it was a must to have hot, boiling water on the open hearth for the plucking of feathers before the final cleaning. I can still remember the unpleasant smells of smoking boiling water and left-over feathers. This stench was awful, but necessary. Thank goodness, the mountain winds quickly swooped the unpleasant odors away from the humble homes. At the end, however, the meal was always delicious!

Depending on the seasons, different foods appeared on the table for consumption by the hungry family. Large, earthen-baked pots surfaced from under the clay hearth to cook the largest squash or pig head for *pozole* (pork and corn kernel soup) and *tamales* or the tasty honeycomb *menudo* (beef stomach-lining soup). During the corn harvest, the fresh kernels were used to make the traditional *uchepus*. For the long hours of cooking the uchepus, thick layers of soot formed always around the pottery ware.

The *uchepus* have to be one of my favorite traditional Mexican foods found in Michoacán. The *uchepus* are a sort of *tamal* wrapped in green corn husks, as opposed to the dried, traditional corn husks used to make the tamales. The sweet mixture of mashed corn, sugar, milk and cinnamon turned into a textured and grainy *masa* (dough) before it was placed between the green husks. The women spent hours folding the delicious smelling, raw *uchepus* before placing them in a clay pot for a vapor-style cooking period. The tasty "*uchepus*" is part of the native foods the Aztecs left for the *Mestizos*. At the time the *uchepus* were made, the corn was freshly cut and ground before it lost its sweet flavors. The sweet-tasting *uchepus* were great with milk or eaten with thick, whole-milk cream.

I fondly remember my mother's special Mexican chocolate made with our own cow's fatty milk. My brothers brought the milk, and my mother used it for many recipes, including delicious hot chocolate. This was not an everyday treat; when milk was not available, she would use water instead. The old Mexican adage, "*como agua para chocolate*," was one of my mother's favorites. If milk was not available for the chocolate, poor families used water, and therefore, "like water for chocolate," was initiated. The taste of chocolate with a water base gave a lighter taste than chocolate made with whole milk. My mother would use this saying whenever we would begin to complain for lacking something or another.

Many of the regional foods requiring fresh ingredients disappeared when we immigrated to the United States. To our discontent, the smell of fresh husks and sweet corn was sorely missed when we first moved to the Imperial Valley. Fresh corn was not readily available in the lower desert lands in the early sixties. Shopping was also done only once a week in the small California town of Calipatria.

The butchering of a pig was perhaps the most colorful event in the traditional preparation of foods in rural México. I clearly remember the discomfort in hearing the pig squealing in agony during the slaughtering process. One side of our village knew when the other side was involved in the butchering of a pig, because the lamenting sounds of the pig echoed against the mountain-side. Once they finished, the men used large hooks and rope to hang the bare carcass of the freshly slaughtered pig so that the men and women could point and pick the parts of the animal for their cooking recipes. Immediately, the butcher would take a huge blade to cut the customer's preferred choice of meat.

As a child, I remember going to the river's edge with piles of full, messy and stinky intestines for cleanup. Once at the river, we took thin sticks to clean the long, skinny and slimy intestines inside-out. The awful smell of pig wastes was unbearable. Once the intestines were cleaned, I remember following the floating remains down the river stream. After the long, skinny tripe was cleaned, the women returned to the kitchen to prepare these thin, tube-like intestines for lunch or dinner. The women would cut the long intestines into smaller pieces, frying them to perfection in their own left-over fatty layer of grease. The fresh *tomatillo* sauce was added after the tripe pieces released enough greasy left-over to mix with the green liquid. This was an extremely delicious treat. A warm tortilla was a perfect blanket to roll with the *tomatillos* based sauce and pieces of the freshly cleaned, fried tripe. The clean and scrubbed tripe was also used for the casing of homemade *chorizo* (sausage). The *chorizo-* making was completed when the stuffed tripe links were properly tied and hung to dry in the heights of the kitchen.

The varieties of foods on the table were more noticeable during the Lenten religious period. My mother made sure that if the Pope had said "no meat," we had no meat. We observed the Catholic rules of the foods we could and could not eat. My mother carefully planned the menus and prepared the ingredients to ensure that we did not eat meat during the Lenten Fridays. She prepared egg-based foods such as "*tortas en caldo de camaron*" (shrimp omelet in soup) and *capirotada* (bread pudding). The delicious *sopa de fideo* (spaghetti and tomato-based soup) was also frequently prepared. My mother's best recipe was that of *arroz de leche* (sweet rice with milk). The cooked rice with sweetened milk was the best dessert the family enjoyed growing up with my mom's cooking.

When we arrived in California, we also missed the fresh cheese available in our small Mexican village. In México, my mother often bought cheese wrapped in green banana tree or Bird of Paradise plant leaves from street vendors. Unlike the yellowish, dry *Cotija* cheese (a popular and famous hard cheese made in the town of *Cotija*, Michoacán), the fresh, white cheese did not crumble. The Mexican cheese was so fresh that it always left droplets of milky colored substance on the leaves.

During the different hunting periods in México, it was not unusual to have fresh rabbit or skinny doves cooked in the green pepper sauce with fried beans and homemade corn tortillas. Flour tortillas were extremely rare to find on our table. Flour was an expensive commodity and therefore not affordable for large and poor families in Mexican villages.

During the early sixties, Mexican food restaurants were not as common as they are today in the United States. This was true even near the border towns in California. Going to a Mexican restaurant was a special occasion for all of us. As a family, we also shared some of our cultural foods with friends and acquaintances. My father's best friend, Teofilo Martinez, occasionally treated us to Mexican food at a well-known restaurant in Brawley, driving us to town in his fancy automobiles.

During our first few years in the United States, we were introduced to many new foods and products. One of the first foods that caught my eye was the white slices of bread served during school lunches. I had never seen white, soft bread and never in such fine and perfect slices. Typical breads in México were made from wheat or corn. Years later, it became common for mom 'n' pop stores to sell Pan Bimbo (Mexican brand of bread) in the small villages. Sandwiches never became a popular food in our new American home. Our mother continued to spoil all of us with hot meals at every occasion. The hot weather in Imperial Valley had lots to do with the changes in our eating habits.

Early on in our new American home, my mother's cooking was sought after by our family friends and work bosses. At my father's request, my mother often cooked special burritos for his bosses at the Rocking Arrow. The burritos became a tradition at the cattle ranch. The burritos were not spicy or hot because my father's palate did not appreciate the spicy and tingling taste of *chile picoso* (hot pepper) in foods. Everything at home was cooked in a non-traditional, Mexican mild but tasty flavor, to suit my father's tastes.

My mother also took pride in inviting the local priests to our family dinners or lunches. She made sure that the finest ironed tablecloth was set on the table. When the priest was to visit, my mother bent over backwards to ensure that the best foods were served. Not only did the table look dressed, we were also expected to dress up for the visit from the priest.

My mother made the fanciest preparations when the priest would visit our home. I don't believe that we considered bringing our pottery dishes from México. Instead, my mother slowly gathered her own set of plates, glasses and silverware. My mother collected the plates occasionally found in the oatmeal boxes. Other times, she would find a cup inside the boxes instead of a saucer.

These incentive gifts in our oatmeal boxes worked! My mother made oatmeal as often as possible, generating a complete set of dishes for the family. Other dishes and glassware came from the two fairs that we visited during the year. We all enjoyed tossing the ten cents, watching the dancing dime land into one of the dishes that eventually ended up in our kitchen.

My mother also was a great "Blue Chip" stamp collector. She took the stamps from the grocery store and pasted them in some special books until she had enough to purchase additional kitchenware. As a child, I was always disappointed that she chose the kitchen stuff instead of the great toys in exchange for the stamps. El Centro, California hosted the stamp exchange location that my mother eagerly visited every time she had filled enough stamp books. Dishes were always on top of the wish list for my mother's stamp collection efforts. Our home was filled with a hodgepodge of dishes and glassware. These were the best dishes we had to serve our special guests. It was only many years later that we bought our first full set of dishes. The priests were served with the oatmeal dishes during their early visits to our home.

During our many years in the Imperial Valley, we knew the arrival and the departure of the different priests of Immaculate Heart of Mary parish in Niland. The tradition in México was to host the priest or nuns to a meal, and our parents did not miss a step in fulfilling their obligation to share our home, our foods and our culture with the local priests. The priests never failed to show up for my mother's great Mexican meals.

In our home, the priest and nuns are always served first, and the rest followed, according to age and family status. One particular memory took place in the early sixties, with the parish priest from Niland joining us for dinner. On this occasion, my mother had prepared a fabulous three or five-course meal for the visiting priest. The house had been swept clean by Blanca on the inside, and Hector was in charge of the outside. My mother and I were in charge of the kitchen, and my father made sure that the drinks were available, including some Port wine. I believe I was also in charge of initiating some type of conversation, since my mother did not speak English and many of the priests did not speak Spanish.

After the blessing, my father began to pass the plates of food for the priest to serve himself in a family-style dinner. All meals with priests included fried rice, some type of meat, a salad and refried beans with tortillas. For this meal, the dessert included fruit and, on this special occasion, gelatin. It was obvious to us that the guest had never visited a Mexican home during meal time. Like an archeologist studying some type of new community, the priest's blue eyes followed every movement of our eating habits, watching and learning as we chewed on foods and warm tortillas. It was obvious that this priest had rarely visited Mexican families, as he watched every detail of our eating habits. Everyone knew tortillas should be served when hot. We never ate cold tortillas. The best tortillas were those that continued to smoke as the heat was released from the tortillas into the palms of our hands.

We rarely used forks growing up. Instead, we cut pieces of the tortilla with our fingers to spoon up some rice or meat in small, chewable amounts. We took the tasty rice and meat from our plates, nestling the ingredients smack in the middle of the corn or flour tortilla. Next, we delicately rolled the tortilla into a tube with the juicy droppings falling on the plate. The priest intently watched our delicious, self-made tacos end up in our hungry mouths.

During the visits by priests, we were to behave and to be polite at all times. While we were not wealthy, our parents wanted the priests to know that we were extremely respectful and well-mannered to the church authority and to the representatives from the Pope. We were always reminded that in our own family, we were blessed with one of our own sisters, a nun, belonging to the Order of the Holy Family in México.

Finally, my mother and sister removed the larger beige plates to make room for the highly anticipated dessert. The dessert, a humble pan of red gelatin with slices of bananas properly stationed on the surface, was placed in front of the priest as he also waited with anticipation to cut into the delicious, cool dessert. The stiffened dish barely trembled as my mother cut a corner piece of the red gelatin with banana for the priest. All of us watched with anticipation as my mother proceeded to cut a piece for our father. For the rest of us, the plate was passed around.

Once the red gelatin sat on every small plate around the table, we waited, as we had been instructed, for the priest to start. He did. He stretched his hand to the small cloth covering of the tortilla dish. Confidently, he took the warm tortilla and placed it in his left hand. The tasty tortilla sat on his long, white fingers while we watched with much amazement. I am certain that my eyes focused solely on the unexpected tortilla.

The priest then proceeded to take his right hand to spoon some gelatin into the tortilla sitting flat on his left hand. He spooned the gelatin onto the tortilla until he had enough for a rolled taco. He made an assumption that we ate tortillas with all foods. We had modeled this behavior by eating our rice and meat with tortillas. Our eyes could not believe that the priest was eating his dessert with a tortilla. Obviously, this was a very funny sight!

We were all giggling inside our stomachs as my mother watched us and with her smart, tiny eyes instructed us to settle down and not say one single word. I remember several of us tapping each other under the table as we muffled our emotions inside our stomachs with a tremendous desire to burst into laughter. The priest continued to eat his gelatin in a taco-like manner until he saw my father use his spoon to eat the tasty dessert. In our home, we were never to point out any mistakes made by our guests.

The priest knew that he was trying to be considerate by making sure he did things the way we did them. He knew that he was doing something silly only after he watched my father and the rest of the family eating the gelatin with our spoons. This evening turned out to be a learning experience for both the priest and the family. After our guest left, we laughed so hard at the funny way of eating gelatin and the humorous ways of the Gringo priest.

The tortilla and gelatin taco conversation lasted long after the priest had visited our home. We all learned a lesson as we saw an outsider with a different cultural orientation eat gelatin with tortillas for the first and last time in his life. Ironically, we did some of the same things in trying to fit into our new home, language and country.

In our Mexican village, we had never heard of such things as the pilgrims, pumpkin pie or Thanksgiving Day. Our early exposure to Thanksgiving came from elementary school. It was strange to hear that everyone had to eat turkey on a Thursday in November. Turkeys were not new to us, since my grandfather had the silly birds in his home. But chopping the turkey into a meal was not done on a specific day when we were growing up.

I suppose drinking raw eggs was strange to Americans too, but the process of preparing a turkey was, in my mind, a horrific task for American women. *Just imagine the plucking of the feathers that the women would have to deal with on the day of Thanksgiving*, I thought.   Obviously, we were naïve about the fast-track modernization of processing animal meat in the United States. I recall my mother laughing when I told her the teacher had instructed us to eat turkey for the festive days of Thanksgiving.

The real lessons of Thanksgiving came later on, when we finally understood the meaning and emotion behind "giving thanks." My brother-in-law Tommy and his family taught my sister María Elena how to cook the featherless, big bird. When I was a child, I remember my sister bringing the cooked turkey to our home. The first time she brought a cooked turkey "American style", I imagined her with a big bag full of wet, plucked turkey feathers left behind in her home of Pico Rivera, California. In those days, we were confused as to the right word for turkey in America. My sister called it *cocono*, *pavo* and *guajolote*. Whatever name was used for the delicious meat, we enjoyed the meal very much.

During our first Thanksgiving in the United States, many foods appeared on the table, bridging the two cultures into one happy family. At our first Thanksgiving luncheon, we had fried Mexican rice, *frijoles*, *tamales*, *tortillas*, pork meat and delicious *guajolote* (turkey).

Our parents always provided plenty of food on the table for all of us. Early on, my mother cooked for an extra-large family, and as we left the home to build our own families, my mother continued to cook in large portions. There was always a pot on the stove with a fresh-cooked, hot dish.

I began to cook with my mother in the early sixties. Blanca, my sister, loved to clean and dust the house. She hated the kitchen chores and disliked cooking. I, on the other hand, despised cleaning house and moving furniture around from one side to the other. I loved helping my mother in the kitchen. I learned to cook with my mother "side by side." I started with the less important chores of cutting tomato and peeling the onions and garlic. My mother enhanced my skills by allowing me to work with the frying of pork meat and chicken rice. My mother never measured any ingredients, and with time, neither did I. It was all in the feel of the food, the smell of the flowing cloud of smoke from the pot and the preliminary taste. Most importantly, I spent more time in the kitchen listening to my mother's soothing voice about everything from her random opinions regarding family to her childhood stories growing up in Tangancicuaro, Michoacán, México.

To this day, I love to cook the Mexican rice from scratch and the pork burritos with a taste of mild *chile* (pepper) sauce. On the dessert side, I learned to cook my mother's special *arroz de leche* with cinnamon and Mexican vanilla. My devoted mother crafted all her meals around the head of the household, my father. When the entire servings were safely in our stomachs, my mother and father were proud and relieved that once again, they were able to provide for us.

The kitchen was a place to hear the latest news about the nine siblings of Silvino and María Zendejas. As the family grew, the kitchen continued to be the source of the good news and sometimes the bad news about *hijos* (sons), *nietos* (grandchildren), *visnietos* (great-grandchildren) and *tatara nietos* (great-great-grandchildren). If the walls of our Mexican kitchens could talk, we would learn much more about our family ancestry.

The use of the *metate* and *molcajete* (stone kitchen tools used for grinding) has disappeared from our kitchens, except for decorative purposes. The occasional use of the *molinillo* (a wooden carved kitchen tool with a bulbous, hollow end) to stir the Mexican chocolate is unique to rural *cocinas* (kitchens) of México.

My mother's gift to all of us was the love that she packed into every meal she served. The kitchen continues to be the place of gathering and sharing the memories of the woman who sacrificed so much for us and throughout the years brought so much love and care through the dishes she prepared for us.

In our family, all gatherings become feasts of Thanksgiving and appreciation for the traditions that bring us together. The busy chatter of our kitchen provides everyone an equal opportunity to chip in their "*cinco centavos*" worth of comments. Perhaps the Zendejas' kitchen was like an open recipe book depicting the entire family. Little did we know that the array of foods served in our kitchen would represent the tapestry of personalities and views within the large, diverse and happy family.

Mom's Humble Remedies

1962

I do not remember ever visiting a doctor's office until we were living in California. In the small Mexican village where we were born, only dying elders and pregnant women delivering babies were given any medical attention. Maximiana, the local midwife, provided the herbs, teas, and poultices used for all our village's medical needs.

When we immigrated to the United States, my mother brought many of the village remedies with her to help us, until she could grow or find what was needed in the new country. Within two years in our new home, my mother was cultivating *manzanilla* (chamomile), *yerba buena* (mint), *malvas* (geraniums), *ruda*, and cactus in the desert garden. Our mother continued with her own techniques to desalinate the Imperial Valley water in order to grow her medicinal plants. She was determined to succeed in growing the plants she needed, and there was no stopping her. Frankly, deep down, everyone admired her grit.

, she saved coffee grounds, egg shells, orange rinds, and
leftovers to transform into her soothing compresses. She had
remedies for most aches and pains imaginable to keep her family
healthy. Our mother created her own kidney-cleansing water and
her own medications for menstrual pains.

The only medication I remember ever taking as a child, both in
México and in California, was the powdered *Pirarjina* (aspirin),
folded neatly in a square piece of paper. It was like working with
an origami design to pull open the tiny flaps of the paper package.
Once the paper was fully spread apart, the white medicine powder
was poured into a glass filled with water, dissolving the contents
before drinking.

Dr. Foster was the first real physician I had ever met. Other
immigrant families went to him because he was willing to help
underprivileged Mexican families. There was always a crowd
waiting to see this kind man. His Brawley, California office was
always painted as white as his lab coat.

However, Dr. Foster is best remembered, at least in my family, for
prescribing castor oil for nearly everything, about which we
complained. Despite his generosity, we hated to visit Dr. Foster,
because we knew what came next. I hated the thick, slimy oil that
left a taste of raw fish in my mouth long after I had swallowed. It
seemed to me that the oil would be best to feed to the cats or other
animals, but not me; it made me go to the bathroom more times
then necessary. My mother said it really cleaned and cleared out

all my innards, and soon it was added to her list of modern home remedies.

We were fortunate in that all of us were generally healthy and rarely needed anything more than one of my mother's special cures. When one of us had an earache, she had just the appropriate remedy for the pain. With her tender hands, she rolled a sheet of newspaper (when my father was finished reading it, of course,) into a huge, ice-cream cone shape. Then she helped the earache-sufferer bend over a table and place his or her head on the flat surface, with the painful ear turned up. The pointed end of the newspaper cone went into the ear canal, and she lit the big end with a match. She was always especially careful to make sure my sister's and my braids were tight and out of the way before she struck the match. Immediately, the newspaper print began to lose its ink into the pouring of smoke.

About the time the newspaper had burned halfway down, a puff of air shot up through the cone opening. It was as if a small volcano puffed its first sign of eruption. Satisfied with the puff of air, my mother immediately removed and extinguished the burning cone, and the earache usually went with it. If the newspaper cone did not cure our pain, she had a second remedy, equally different from the popular pink penicillin (Amoxicillin) liquid found in most families' refrigerators to treat childhood ear infections.

My mother's garden was filled with many natural remedies. For ear infections, she picked some *malva* (geranium) leaves and placed them on the hot *comal* (a flat pan for cooking tortillas). She grilled the leaves until they were hot and then added a few drops of water to make them mushy. Using her index finger and thumb, she rolled the cooked, green leaves into a small ball. We did not mind having our ears plugged with the warm, green leaves. Whenever she did this to me, I pretended I could not hear, so I could get away with doing my own thing and not taking any orders for additional chores.

As a child, I was proud of my mother, because I thought she knew a great deal about medicine. It turns out that she knew a great deal about caring for her family with minimal intrusion from modern medicine. She had her own ways of caring for herself, too. At a young age, I helped her drop beeswax tears from a candle onto her toes. Bothersome calluses and *juanete* (bunions) had built up that caused her pain after a long day on her feet. During the evenings, I sat at her feet like a gentle servant and helped tilt the flame of the candle, aiming tiny pearls of beeswax on her dry, yellowing skin. She said the warm wax made her feel good, and that having her youngest child help her made it even better. A firm and careful approach was needed to aim the hot wax droplets directly at the spots where she wanted them, much like guiding an airplane to a smooth landing. When the hot drops of wax touched her skin, the entire foot twitched from the unusual sensation.

Helping to cure my mother's corns was exciting to me as a child, because I could play with the wax, too. After each hot drop fell on her skin, I had to wait a few minutes until it cooled and she was ready for another. In the meantime, I poured extra drops on my hands and quickly molded tiny birds and flowers. I could understand why the wax made my mother feel good. The wax felt good even on my soft, callousness less hands. The wax formed a tiny tortilla, quickly cooling. I often got carried away, and the wax ended up landing on the furniture or the floor. My mother and I often made tiny wax figures with the warm and soft leftover wax, once her feet had been treated.

My mother began to develop gray clouds over her pupils during the early 1970s, when I was in college. She told me that in México, green *tomatillos* (small green tomatoes covered by dry leaves) were used to cure cataracts. My mother boiled *tomatillos* and strained them through cheesecloth, then lay down and had me place the cheese-cloth over her eyes. She rested calmly until the cloth had cooled. She repeated this procedure almost weekly, and for many years was able to keep the cataracts from growing. The same gray clouds appeared again shortly before her passing. It was as if she wanted me to recall the happy memories that we shared with the boiled green *tomatillos*.

All children have fevers on occasion, and ours were treated in a special way by our mother. After we had gone to bed for the evening, my mother gathered coffee grounds, petroleum jelly, and smelly ointments. She mixed the ingredients in the middle of several sheets of newspaper, and then folded the newspaper into shoe shapes. She tied the mushy *plantillas* (soles) to the bottoms of our feet, like summer sandals, with long, thin strips torn from old rags. By the time we woke up the next morning, the unusual poultice had worked its magic on our pain and fever. We used to laugh when she so tenderly applied these mushy shoes to the older brothers. These silly, homemade footings looked funnier on my grown brothers with big feet, who hated these things on their feet. My mother took her remedies extremely seriously, unlike the receivers of such warm and temporary tender care. The ridiculous, soft homemade footwear always worked miracles.

Every home remedy always involved a specific process that almost guaranteed positive results. These remedies were graciously welcomed as the best-choice medicine. In our home, it was common to see the brothers lying on their aching backs, while my mother worked on the remedy for the sharp pain. The preparation was strange, but curious and interesting. My mother obtained a tiny candle and a large coin, along with a clean glass. My mother's hands surveyed the area of pain and began the procedure to cure the ailment. The candle was lighted as it sat on the base of the Mexican coin. The coin and candle were placed on the back. As soon as the coin was firmly set on the skin, the small, clear glass was turned upside-down over the flame. Immediately, our childhood eyes popped wide open with amazement at the skin rising like magic into the opening of the glass. The red, swollen skin resembled a ball protruding from under the skin. The *ventosa* (cupping) was completed when the flame sucked in all the possible oxygen in the glass and from the skin. A large, red spot was left over on the skin for days to come, but miraculously, the back pain was gone.

When I began to have menstrual cramps at age fifteen, my mother had a remedy for such discomfort. At my first complaint, my mother sent me off to bed and prepared the *comal*, heating several tortillas to a toasty degree. Pulling back the bed covers, she raised my clothing to expose my belly, covered it with a warm tortilla, and then wrapped me back up like a baby papoose. The tucking of the blankets under the sides of my body are lasting memories of care and love. The tortillas were great for tacos, but even better on certain days for other purposes. In later years, she tenderly ironed towels to place them over our bellies, while the pain settled and disappeared. During my college days, one of the senior resident students laughed when I asked if she had a great, big flour tortilla and a warming pan to cure my ills. I sure missed my mother's simple ways to tend the pains and ills of the body during the early college days.

As my mother grew older, she would store her homemade remedies in the refrigerator. I can still see the jar filled with a yellowing, tea-like liquid made from boiled corn silk. She always told me that someday, I would also boil the corn silk to clean my kidneys and to work through any urinary infections. My mother, in her own ways, prepared us for the day that she would no longer be able to help us through our ills and pains.

It probably was not the remedies, but my mother's tender care that made us well. She rubbed our feet as if they were her own and made special chicken soup on the days that we were forced to stay in bed. Her kind eyes followed our every move for any sign of discomfort. She inquired about our pain to see what she could do to help with whatever pain existed. Perhaps it was because she took such good care of us that we rarely complained about pains and ills to her or to the rest of the family.

It always seemed to me that just the touch of her hand could make any pain go away. I knew it was the nature of being our mother that brought this special touch to our family. A soft touch and a smile from our mother cured many childhood ailments.

Popcorn

1959

In the late 1950s, we did not have boxed televisions or video games to distract us from games and other outdoor activities available all four seasons. We happily and naturally stretched our imaginations under the sunny Mexican skies in the fresh floral air. La Yerbabuena, like many other villages in México, did not have electricity to run the so-called *aparatos* (apparatus) or equipment with motors.

Girls my age played make-believe housewives and mothers, using tiny pottery dishes and miniature pots to serve food made from local plants. Tiny flowers resembling miniature broccoli florets were picked and served for the pretend lunch. We collected dry pieces of wood for a small fire large enough to cook the spinach-green herbs in the pottery. We called it *caquita de gallina* (chicken manure) which had a tart taste of spinach and collard greens. We carried tiny *papier-mâché* dolls wrapped in *rebosos* (shawls), emulating the women in our village, who usually had several children at an early age. Expectations for young girls were minimal then. The subtle message we got was, *"Grow up, get married, and have as many children as you can because they are a blessing to the family."*

During the month of May, the village celebrated the holiest of mothers, Mary. On weekdays young girls dressed as *almas gloriosas* (glorious souls) to honor Mary. We wore our lacy white communion dresses for this special occasion. The girls and their mothers prepared for the celebration by carefully plucking the petals from the beautiful, fresh garden flowers. The prepared petals were placed in baskets to take to the evening mass.

We carried our fragrant baskets, floating toward the church like angels on feathery clouds. During the mass, we politely tossed the petals high toward the priest, who stood at the base of the altar. The colorful pastel petals rained down like confetti against the priest's white robes. Every young girl who had taken her first communion in the Catholic Church looked forward to the excitement of being part of this religious celebration. This was probably one of the few times that girls were permitted to be part of the religious celebration outside the role-playing of live nativity scenes.

When girls and boys played together, the activities were different. Having so many brothers, I remember watching them play with lots of dirt, so I followed in their footsteps. I created tiny mud hills, using the bottom indentations of empty tequila bottles. We

then made the tiny structures of soft mud burst apart by lighting
wax matches into the center of the mound, causing a few
entertaining seconds of small levy-breaking. The feel of soft mud
in our young hands was a remarkable childhood experience.

Mud playing was normal pastime for children in our small village,
especially during the rainy season. Playing with mud was also
work for grown-ups. Older men used their feet in mixing straw
and earthen clay to form the perfect gelatinousness consistency for
making the adobe blocks for the humble homes. The men did half
of the work; the Mexican sun did the rest.

The mixing of the ingredients with clay was fun to watch as older
men danced in their shoeless feet, mixing the yellow straw with
slippery clay. This process was a team effort as other men
carefully poured the right amount of water into the center of the
action. I fondly remember the fun times watching the wet mud on
the feet and calves of the dancing men. This was truly a sight to
treasure. To avoid the mess, the working men rolled the leggings
of their pants up above the knee for the entire mixing period. As
the men rested, the hot Aztec sun dried the light layer of mud
below the knees. During this process, the mud would turn
different shades of colors on the feet and legs of the men.

Just as the bakers know when the bread is baked, the men knew
when the mud mixture was just right for the sun to do the rest.
Once the perfect consistency was reached, the men poured the
thickened mixture into the rectangular wooden molds. The hot

sun rays then baked the mud recipe into hardened adobe blocks used for building the home structures in our village. The hot sun always worked miracles for the poor.

The women also worked with mud to beautify their homes. They used their hands to add fresh layers of mud to the adobe walls of the homes in our village. The *enjare* (new layer of fresh mud over the adobe clay walls) made the home smell like the fragrant and humid earth, yet clean. The women took galvanized buckets filled with soft mud to begin their work. With their hands, the women would spread the light mud over the parts of the walls in need of sprucing up. Once the home was given another coat of mud, the appearance improved significantly. The early reminder of the *enjare* process came to mind the first time we were asked to finger-paint. The *enjare* and finger-painting processes shared many similarities. During finger-painting time in elementary grades, I imagined myself working among the women in our small village.

Sometimes, we climbed into the dark attic of one of our homes to spy on all the people passing by on the cobblestone street below. Many perfect eye-holes were created by the uneven placement of the adobe mud blocks holding the rustic wood beams. Tiny cracks in the tile roof allowed sun rays to shine their spotlights on us. The straight, bright lines formed by the sun were filled with particles of corn dust rising from the latest harvest safely stored. We sat in the attic for what seemed like hours, just watching the people pass by, laughing because they did not know they were being seen.

My favorite of all childhood activities was making and eating *chivitas* (popcorn) during the dry season from October to April. I never could have imagined then that the *chivitas* treat one day would take just a few minutes to cook behind the glass doors of a microwave oven. Our popcorn required a team effort and a long time to make. Our outdoor popcorn activity was laborious, but filled with fun and anticipation.

It was not the usual type of kernel that produced the chewy, white treat, so one of the children took responsibility for bringing the special corn. We divided into groups to help make the fire. The younger ones of the group were directed by the older children to collect enough long, dry sticks for everyone. And the most important task was to gather many dried cow chips; the neatly rounded ones worked the best. Others were often tossed skyward for the fun of watching them fall to the ground and break into a thousand pieces. These cow chips resembled the burnt tortillas that were often tossed to the dogs for a meal. The cow chips, when dried, were heavy. When tossed, the chips did not glide as well as the plastic Frisbees of today. Instantly after a few feet of flight, the dried manure hit the hard ground to begin the next cycle of fertilizing the wildflowers that grew year-round in the hills.

Some of the cow chips sported grayish mushrooms. Other chips landed on the large, volcanic rocks in the cows' path and dried against them, making them nearly impossible to use. Still others had large hoof prints, creating large craters in the middle of the cow pie. The best cow chips were those that had been deposited flat on the ground like huge chocolate-chip cookies. Nature had a way of making these things just perfect for our popcorn-making needs.

After everyone had gathered the required natural supplies, the older children took over. The assembled cow chips were organized into an architectural structure resembling a pyramid, with the larger ones supporting the base of the pile and the tiny chips made by the calves placed carefully on the top. One of the older boys always brought the matches, which were made of a soft, waxy substance and tipped with bright-red phosphorus. He lit a few matches to ignite the dry sticks that were layered in with the manure. The small fires were started at each of the four cardinal points to make sure the cow chip pyramid burned evenly. The rest of us waited eagerly to watch the fire burn down. As the cow chips began to fall into the center of the pile, we knew it was almost time for the popcorn.

Our excitement was contagious as the cow chips began to burn in fierce colors of red, orange and blue. When the fire turned bright amber, one boy poured the kernels into the center of the burning pile, and another began to fold the hot manure over the kernels with two of the long sticks we had gathered. When the corn was completely covered, the boy used two long sticks to pound the manure more evenly over the smoking kernels. This was the last step before the tiny, white-winged doves of corn began to emerge, jumping out from the hot, dusty mixture.

We all cheered when the first kernel jumped out. Like magic, the *chivitas* exploded from under the dusty manure. Each of us used a long stick to kick the hot kernels out of the fire and into our hands, and then quickly popped them into our mouths. There was always more than we could eat. The *chivitas* were so good that we did not need butter or salt to enhance their flavor. The dusting of burned cow manure added a wonderful natural taste.

The popping continued for several minutes before we moved on with our full and happy stomachs. The patch of scorched ground was the only evidence left as a reminder of our fun. Thanks to the cows, the corn harvest, and a little country ingenuity, we made our own brand of popcorn. Today, every time I hear the familiar popping sounds combined with the smell of buttered, cooked corn coming from a microwave oven, I smile and remember the more natural ways of the past. I hope someday I will have a chance to repeat and cherish the delicious popcorn recipe inspiring great childhood memories.

Critters

1958

In the 1950's, the women of our rural Mexican village gathered for a social hour with an unusually productive outcome. After their morning chores of making tortillas by hand and preparing *almuerzo* (late breakfast), on certain days women escaped outside to sit together on the large, porous volcanic rocks, to talk and *espulgar* (de-lice) themselves.

They patiently unraveled each other's long, black braids, their bronze or white skin shining in the sun's bright rays as they tilted their heads to help loosen their hair. A symphony of work-worn hands orchestrated the flowing motions that released the tight plaits. Most women had long hair woven into an intricate pattern. During most of the day, they covered their heads with long *rebosos* (shawls) of assorted colors. The *rebosos* were also very useful during the important childrearing time for the women. The women wrapped their babies in a bundle held next to their warm bellies. The *rebosos* were particularly convenient for hiding the full breast of the mothers feeding their young.

The younger women wore *rebosos* of lighter-colored material. Many of the older women wore mourning rebosos in dark colors. These *rebosos* were an indispensable part of everyday dress in the Mexican village.

With the *rebosos* removed from their heads, the women took turns digging through each other's thick hair in search of *piojos* (lice), using their index and middle fingers to part it down to the scalp. They showed young girls like me how to remove lice, as if this knowledge helped us to become successful grownups. The village had a pestilence of lice, and everyone knew it. By removing the lice, we made life simpler.

At last, one of the women found a louse and picked it out with agile fingers, placing it on the nail of one thumb. Before the parasite's last breath, the women brought the bug close to their faces as if to look it in the eye before the attack. At the same time, the opposite hand swooped in, and the *piojo* would die mercilessly. Its size could be measured by the tone of the popping sound it made as it was smashed between two thumbnails. I was fascinated by this entire systemic, team-work process, but my mother was not too happy with my fascination.

This activity provided the women an opportunity to discuss personal subjects they might not share with the men or in front of the men. This gathering gave the younger women a chance to talk about some of the young men in the village. This simplistic process was also a social activity for the women of our village.

After an hour or so of thorough searching and conversation, the women expertly rebraided each other's long, dark hair. The younger women ended with two long braids resembling two long rivers originating behind the ears. The older women with graying and thinning hair usually ended with one long, gray braid pointing straight to the tail bone. Most of the women took their *rebosos* and swung them back over their heads before wrapping the ends around the neck and over the back of their shoulder blades. As they casually tossed their shawls over their shoulders, the women armed themselves with confidence and security in who they were and what they did. They resembled soldiers with marching orders as they proceeded in their routines for the day. In some ways, I suppose that is exactly what the women did. Instead of going to war, however, these women went about their daily chores in a dedicated manner, determined to fulfill the duties required of many of them, while their husbands, fathers, brothers and sons were off to *El Norte* to work the fields for a modest living in México. A long day awaited the women of this small town. The morning chit-chat for the Mexican women of this village resembled the modern-day gathering of women at the local book store, complete with conversation, coffee and literature.

Just before we left México to live in the United States, a group of men dressed in outfits resembling Apollo men on the moon came with orders from the government to kill all the *piojos, chinches, garapatas and pulgas* (lice, bedbugs, ticks and fleas) in the village. They created a lunar ambiance with their equipment, pure white outfits and white, full head coverings. It was as if the "Pied

Piper" had arrived to drive all the critters to the wild river of the village. Most villagers were more concerned with the rats and mice than they were with the non-threatening *piojo*. The families had to hide their piles of corn in the *sotabanco* (attic), concealing them from the starving mice. Besides, in the land of machismo, most of the *piojo*s were found in women. I always thought that *piojo*s did not like big sombreros, and so they stayed away from men. The few bald men in the village did not worry about *piojos*.

At the time of the spraying of the white dust, all of us were asked to leave our mud homes for a few days. We were ordered to cover all food for an entire day or so. Most importantly, the corn in the attic had to be brought down and out, for the poison sprayed could harm the dry corn. Much work was done to ready the homes for the coming of the Apollo men. With tanks attached to their bodies, the foreign outsiders sprayed a powdery white fumigant, its escaping particles clearly visible in the air under the bright Mexican sun. The particles of the fumigant were so different from the volcanic dust particles that had consumed the village in 1943 after the eruption of the cornfield volcano, *Paricutín*.

All of the villagers slept outside, including my family. My mother was on top of all the household matters. She made sure that enough tortillas and cooked beans were made the day before. Tortillas, beans, cheese, milk and eggs sufficed for these few days. This minor inconvenience felt more or less normal to the villagers, since nobody had electricity or running water to miss. Our drinking water was stored in clay pot *cántaros* (jugs) resting under a small, overhead tile roof.

The coyotes in the nearby hills could be heard mourning for the *piojo*s and mice that never saw the light again. In the middle of the night, an occasional donkey joined the fatiguing cries for the loss of life in the village. It seemed to me that the non-humans knew that a piece of culture and life was leaving the village; for others, this was progress.

We helped our grandfather, Chano, who was sick with Parkinson's disease. He was taken outside to sit in his wooden chair, close to the rock fence by the chicken coop. As happy as larks, we ate corn tortillas filled with refried beans that had been cooked over an open flame. In the evening, the fireflies added to the wondrous sparks, bringing the stars closer to the people. For two days, the village probably could have qualified for the *Guinness Book of World Records* for the largest slumber party ever held in a small village of México. For our young minds, these events were enchanting, and only many years later did we recognize the last special days and the magic of our village.

Another insect that contributed to the discomfort of our standard of living in México was the *pulga* (flea). Fleas lived on the many dogs, cats, and chickens in our village. On occasion, they also shared our beds.

As far as I was concerned, the worst type of flea was found on chickens, because it was the most difficult one to see and catch. As the youngest in the family, I had the chore of gathering eggs from the chicken coop — a real flea market. As soon as I climbed into the coop, I could feel my feet itching from the invisible bugs that hopped onto my ankles. Sometimes the urge to scratch my legs was overwhelming, and on occasion I dropped an egg or two and got in trouble with my mother.

The worst of all the critters for me was the tick. The *garapata* (tick-literally "grab the foot") was found on many animals in México. I remember seeing these pests on dogs, cats, cows, steers, and horses, and also on people. The vision of these animals sucking the tail end of the cows was overwhelming. I once had one stuck in my ear, just like the cows grazing in the pasture.

One parasite took up residence in my right ear and went unnoticed until I began to scratch compulsively. My mother noticed my unusual effort to stick my entire hand in my ear and realized what was wrong. The tick must have been tiny when it moved in, but now its blood-filled stomach had swelled to fill my ear canal. My mother took me outside, placing my head on her lap so that a ray of Aztec sun served as a spotlight into my ear. She poked at the lazy, fat critter with a needle, but could not burst it. Next, she filled my ear with rubbing alcohol mixed with a few drops of tequila, hoping to intoxicate the bug to the point that it loosened its grip on me; when that did not work, she fried some leaves from one of her medicinal plants and stuck them in my ear. The combined efforts worked, and the tick began to relax. My mother went back to poking its belly with a hot needle, and then I felt a wet rush of warmth in my ear. She pulled the deflated tick from my ear and laid it on a small, flat rock. It looked like a miniature balloon that had been punctured, releasing its air until it landed, shriveled to a wrinkled nothing.

The critters and parasites also lived inside the stomachs of the village children; as in my case. I hosted a nasty *lombriz* (tapeworm) that thrived in my intestine for a long time. My mother said that I had a "*solitaria*" in my tummy. The parasite created a significant craving for cookies during this period of my childhood. The long worm was pulled out by my mother during a visit to the outhouse.

My mother always recalled grabbing the *lombriz* and pulling it out from my body. I was just about four years old at the time of this incident. She told me that I loved to eat *galletas Marias* (a brand of Mexican cookies). I made it a point to sneak as many of these cookies into my mouth as possible. I fondly remember my mother telling this story and laughing at the same time. I am sure that at the time, this was no laughing matter. During the times my mother vividly retold this story, it gave the listeners the impression that she had a wriggle-type of "tug-of-war" with the long and slimy parasite.

My mother always reminded me of the tapeworm's preferred meal, cookies. She said it was a long one, made up of sections shaded the same color as those of my favorite cookies. The worm grew by inching itself longer with each cookie I ate. It was as if the mischievous creature waited for every cookie that I swallowed.

On the eventful had day, my mother was surprised at the size of the parasite that enjoyed living in my innards. I am certain my mother is still looking down on me laughing out loud at these endearing and unforgettable childhood moments.

Long after the masked outer-space men visited our village with their spraying equipment, the women no longer searched each other's hair for lice. A significant decrease in the population of *piojo*s, *pulga*s, *garapatas* and *ratones* had resulted from this strange intervention. The most notable impact however, was the decrease in the number of beautiful, lighted fireflies. During the time of candle burning and moonlight, the fireflies offered a spectacle every night. The burning of the fireflies' bellies of indigo and magenta shades created many poetic nights. With the coming of brighter lights, the poetic nights have turned to television and loud radios on the cemented streets of today. The obnoxious critter today is a type of "pincher bug" drawn by the glaring, electric lights.

Years later, we revisited the lice theme. In elementary school in Niland, California my sister was told she had lice. The school nurse and teachers made such a fuss over her long hair that my mother and father were embarrassed. We did not have lice at home, so someone in the school must have shared their parasitic burden with my sister. My parents worried that she would not be allowed to return to school, and so my mother returned to the old ways, spending several hours searching through and cleaning my sister's thick hair. The special de-lousing shampoos had not been

developed yet. My mother tried everything to get rid of the lice. Many years later, my mother added petroleum to the list of remedies for stubborn head-lice.

Ticks were not as much of a problem in the United States, because animals did not coexist with the family as they had in México, and our home was not so open to the outdoors. Nevertheless, we dealt with them often when we lived near a feedlot. The cattle and horses always had ticks, and pulling them off was a chore we all accepted. The ticks were tough to remove, but eventually our fingers grew sensitive to the correct way. My mother made sure that we changed our clothes after spending time near the animals.

In the Imperial Valley, I spent many hours playing with the red ants that thrived in the hot desert weather. Hundreds of ants removed small gravel and sand from their deep underground homes. Toward the end, the ants were such pests that my father began pouring white powder on the ground to stop their new dwellings from sprouting near our home.

I attribute much of my strong sense of childhood curiosity to growing up in the country with friendly animals. I learned much about science and behavior from the chickens, donkeys, cows, horses, dogs and other critters who lived among us. I played outside as much as possible, seeking the company of my mother or siblings only when the distant coyote howled under the darkening skies.

Another magical insect moment took place while I was listening to the radio in the early sixties. I was suddenly taken by surprise when I heard the musical composition of the *piojo* and the *pulga* (lice and flea). Being that in the United States the radio was one of our in-house forms of entertainment, I was pleasantly surprised to hear "Cri Cri's" (famous children's song writer often compared to Walt Disney) song "El *Piojo* y *La Pulga.*" The song created the image of the wedding between the two. Even today, this song brings to life the warm and pleasant memories of the special country environment in our Mexican village. We ought to be concerned with the possibility that they may someday no longer exist.

My childhood experiences with lice, fleas, and ticks have helped me peacefully coexist with insects as an adult. Nature really never modernizes. Nature adjusts to the modern world in its own unique ways. The insects of today seem to be no different from those that I encountered as a child. There is a level of comfort that I feel knowing that these critters still exist in our high-tech world. In a magical way, these small animals connect me to my roots, to my rural background and to the warm memories of my family. I am convinced that their existence has nurtured many a child like me.

Rocking Arrow Ranch

1960 - 1968

My father immigrated us to the southwestern United States in 1960. Our immigration papers were handed to us by American authorities at the port of entry in Calexico, California. Before we settled in the Imperial Valley, we lived on the Mexican side of the border, while our official documents were being processed. The hot summer in Mexicali was a drastic change from our green mountain village home in Central México. While in Mexicali, we lived in a shanty cement block home located by a dusty road in the sprawling city.

My mother made sure that during our required visits to the immigration offices on the Mexicali and Calexico border, we were neatly dressed, pressed and overall well-groomed. She dressed my sister and me in our best clothes and combed our hair as if we were going to a church event. My father wanted us to make a positive and lasting impression on the *Gringos* (a term used south of the border for Americans) so that our immigration process would be more seriously considered; we could then become residents of the United States. My father firmly believed that if we looked very nice and decent, the authorities would be more understanding of our efforts. Actually, when we were living in México, there were three words that were introduced to us to refer to the people of the United States of America. The most proper name was that of "*Americanos*," followed by "*Gringos*" and "*Gabachos*." As I child, I did not know the meaning of these words. By a certain age, we all knew that the politically correct term to use was "*Americanos*." We also learned that the *Americanos* had words to describe those of us that had come to the new land.

Once we got our first permit to cross into the land of the "fortunate," we were instructed not to return to México until all of our appropriate documents had been signed and delivered. During these times, my father continued to travel into México to buy Mexican goods and to get his regular haircut. My mother, sister and I would walk through all the streets of downtown Calexico. We were all very fond of the Kress Store located on the central street of Calexico. Inside this special store, the fresh smell of popcorn and the chirping live birds were the most enticing reasons to visit Calexico. The Kress Store had a downstairs section filled with my mother's favorite, sewing materials. Once inside, the shiny wooden floors made sure that everyone knew we were coming.

No longer could we wake to the sun slowly flowing over the

mountain onto our enclave mountain village. No longer could we stretch our vista to catch the slow-moving burros and recently milked cows across the hills. The view of the city was filled with dust and old cars passing at unexpected speeds. The scenes of the growing fields of corn, beans and squash were exchanged for tall wooden poles supporting thick, black electrical wires, crossing over the busy streets and diving into the homes. The constant lights in the night were far more glaring than the Mexican fireflies or the soft-spoken candlelight of our adobe home back in the village. Instead, layers of "Pincher bugs" solught the glare of the dazzling lights. The once-visible display of stars and constellations in the night sky were traded for bright headlights and lamps filled with buzzing, dizzy bugs and mosquitoes.

My father, a farm laborer, visited us during the weekend, bringing several brown bags filled with American groceries for the week's needs. Besides the extreme weather and bustling city environmental surroundings, the manner in which food reached our table incited our curiosity. Milk in our small village came early in the morning from the udders of the white, black and brown cows. Our village cows were escorted to milking and feeding areas by my older brothers. In-between the milking times, the cows leisurely passed the time chewing the mountain grass and breathing the fresh air. When we arrived at the big city, milk was sold in strange glass containers. Most other dry goods were in boxes and paper sacks. The morning run to the corn mill was not necessary in the Mexicali and Imperial Valleys. Tortillas were sold at the store, and fresh tortillas were made from bagged, powdered corn meal, *Maseca*. These were not the only changes in our new home. We also had to get used to turning the lights on and off. In our Mexican village, a simple gesture- our breath blowing out the candle- would do. In Mexicali, the magic of lights was switched on and off by a tiny chain of metal-like rosary beads attached to the fixture.

In the Imperial Valley, it was not necessary to take the donkeys to bring the fresh drinking water from the natural spring; the water came to us. Hundreds of canals carried water from the Colorado River to feed the hungry agricultural fields of the Valley. Our home took the water from the Lateral M canal. Every so often, a thick tin gate would be pulled up to facilitate water flow into our small home reservoir. An electric water pump, surrounded by silly wires hanging left and right, sucked the water from the canal into the cemented reservoir. Our washing and showering water came from the canal. Since there were no purification processes or chlorinated systems in our country home, our showers offered a tint of fish smell charging through the old water pipes. Our drinking water in the desert came from the Triple AAA Company. Men delivered drinking water to our home in enormous tanks. The men, dressed in green khaki outfits with red or blue embroidered letters marking them as Triple AAA employees, pulled large hoses to fill our container with the sweet water. The drinking water container sat high on wooden stilts with a single pipe poking into the kitchen window. An old fashioned faucet brought the drinking water right into the kitchen.

To ease any shock of transition, our family began and ended our days as we always had, listening to Mexican music on the radio before the sun came up and praying the rosary together each evening in front of our dressy, homemade altar. The corners in our homes always made better altars, creating an architectural ambiance for the candles and small saint statues. A small wooden table served as the base of the homemade altar. My mother dressed the religious statues with green, red, and white crêpe paper. Sometimes, my mother cut out tiny robes made of left-over materials for our patron saints. The burning candle was a constant reminder of our faith and our unforgettable traditions from México. Somehow, our faith solidly entwined our present with our past.

These rituals gave us a strong sense of family and God that kept our spirits together, even as we knew that we had a long way to go to succeed in the United States. During our early transition into the new environment, we attended Niland Elementary School, located approximately five country miles from the Rocking Arrow Ranch, our new home.

All of us — even I, the youngest — had responsibilities at the bustling Rocking Arrow Ranch, where my father was employed. The symbol of the "rocking arrow" was an immediate imprint of the economy in rural America. Early on, this economy touched and bent our family's expectations and beliefs.

Opportunities there provided us with important lessons about our new culture that we could not have learned so quickly elsewhere. The ranch was filled with exciting and new things for all of us. My brothers also worked at the busy cattle feedlot. The women — my mother, sister, and I — cleaned the ranch offices Sunday through Friday, and at the end of the month, we received a check for twenty-eight dollars. I suppose that was reasonable pay for cleaning in those days. I know that my parents counted on every penny of that check to make ends meet.

By eight o'clock or earlier each evening, we had the place spotless. We focused especially on the business offices, where visitors were welcomed by an enormous set of steer horns mounted right above the entry of the main meeting room. The front room had a large, skyscraper-view window. Executive and spacious leather chairs were arranged around a dark walnut table. From this vantage point, the owners could watch the feedlot men at work and the comings and goings of the cowboys. The one bathroom and a vault-like room were also on our housekeeping list.

My brothers helped collect the trash and do other "boy" chores, ones which I inherited later on. The boys rarely picked up a broom or a mop — that was "girl" work for my sister and me, who occasionally danced with the brooms, pretending we were Cinderella at the American ball or just playing around to help the time move faster. But there was not much time for play. My mother was in charge and made specific assignments known. At first, mine were simple chores — wiping the ashtrays as big as toilet bowls and emptying the black metal trash cans in each of the offices. The feedlot owners left many cigar butts for us to throw away. The large ash trays were always filled with the remnants of huge, half-chewed Cuban cigars. The awful stench of the tobacco lingered in our noses when the trays were emptied. I usually kept my chin close to my shoulders and away from the plume of dust caused by the emptied ashes. I would not be surprised if over the span of the eight years we wiped the equivalent of an entire crop of Southern tobacco from the ashtrays.

The most stimulating times associated with cleaning the feedlot offices came around Christmas, and the most awful time to clean was after Thanksgiving. The bathroom in particular was horrible the Friday and Saturday after the much-celebrated turkey day. My brothers and sisters marveled at the after-Thanksgiving mess, but never really understood the reasons for it until many years later. Thanksgiving was not a known celebration in rural México and not known to us when we first arrived in the Imperial Valley.

During summer, the 100-plus degrees of dry, lower-desert heat made working inside the air-conditioned feedlot offices especially enjoyable. Our home, on the other hand, had old-fashioned water coolers. These boxed motors provided the only relief from the hot, hot summers. The steel coolers contained dry grass filters that helped circulate water, cooling the hot air from the outside as it was sucked into the inside of the home. At our home, the coolers were louder than a jumbo jet taking off from O'Hare; nevertheless, during the hot nights, everyone wanted to sleep in front of the noisy motor. The loud huffing and puffing of the cooler did not interfere with our celebratory nights or deep dreams.

The feedlot office was for us like an oasis in the middle of the desert. The modern air-conditioner poking through a hole cut in the building felt good when we positioned our faces smack in front of the outpouring cold air ducts. A brief, refreshing moment was welcomed at the feedlot office.

A bright red Coca-Cola machine stood at attention in the outside hallway, waiting for every dime we could find to drop into its cold body. This Coke machine meant business, and the need to market the product was minimal. The hot weather made a formidable public relations effort for the Coke machine. In the summer, the bottles pulled from the machine were partially frozen. The refreshing chill from the small bottle of soda was the ultimate reward for our hard work. Getting someone to treat us to a "Coca" was a real treat.

In those days, the cattle industry was energized by prosperity. The Rocking Arrow had grown from a few hundred head of cattle to fifteen thousand, operating from a self-contained, isolated ranch five miles away from the closest elementary school. The feedlot was surrounded by fields of different crops, depending on the season. Several of the crops changed colors during different times of the year, nearly matching the beauty of the changing of the fall leaves in a four-season region. During certain times, it seemed that the Imperial Valley was dressed and adorned in a green alfalfa outfit, sensually swaying with the winds arriving from the south.

An iron grain mill sat next to the ranch's large steel silos, from which huge tubes delivered fodder from the various storage bins to the electric turbines. An enormous sheet-metal roof, protecting the entire process from wind and rain, covered both the electric mill and the rectangular bales of green alfalfa and yellow hay where they sat on a cemented platform. From five in the morning until late afternoon, during the winter months, the loud turbines of the grain mill could be heard inside our home. During the summer months, the water coolers drowned every sound from the mill and stopped any sneaky mouse from risking a dashing moment from one corner of the house to another.

During certain times of the year, the early morning buzz of the crop-dusters painted the soft blue skies with plumes of hazy yellow colors. As they dropped their cargo of pesticide on the flat fields, like pollen, the wind took the odor to the different corners of our home. Whenever the goggled crop duster pilot caught a glimpse of us from the house, he would wave as we marveled at the wonders of flight.

At the southernmost corner of the feedlot, a huge pile of mashed grains and molasses sat growing old and yeasty. My father often pinched a small bit of the cattle feed and ate it himself just to prove to us that it was safe and nutritious. He encouraged us to try different things without being intimidated and eating cattle feed was one more thing he wanted us to try. My mother was a little more reserved about trying this animal feed. My father's facial expressions were stoic until after our first bite, and then he laughed out loud, as if he were proud of us for taking the simple risk and following his instructions. The sweet molasses mix tasted like sugar cane dipped in brown sugar. The woody stalks were soft and juicy. This must have been the steer's favorite casserole.

From time to time, my father used a tractor to move the juicy mixture into large mixing bins. The warm smell of the sweet, fermented air emanated from the pile. From a distance, the silage resembled a pile of dirt. The brewing of the mix continued throughout the time we lived near the feedlot. I suppose this pile of goods was not only for the cattle; the birds, mice and other animals enjoyed the sweet-tasting grass, stalks and grains.

All day long, the feeding truck drove slowly along the dirt road outside the cattle corrals, dumping the mixture of silage and vitamins my father had proudly mixed. The mixture churned out from the side of the truck, with sharp, shiny silver blades turning and slowly dishing out the feed. The prepared feed fell into a cement channel that ran along the outside edge of the corral. The huge bulls and steers poked their heads and maneuvered their cut horns between thick wires to eat the daily meal. Mammoth-sized blood- sucking *tábanos* (horse flies) flew only centimeters away from large eyes, ears and backbones of the complacent animals before landing. The busy *tábanos* forced the tails of the steers to move back and forth like the long pendulum of a grandfather's clock. It was evident by the casual steers' flying tails that they wanted to prevent the *tábanos* from taking their blood. Simply, the steers had their own ecosystem with the insects, bugs and birds around them.

To supply the steers with salt, each corral had a block of salt for licking. The wear and tear on the square salt blocks appeared as smooth indentations on the top and sides. The steers were not embarrassed to stick their long tongues out, swiping the block of tasty salt several times in a row. The sound of the licking was as if soft sandpaper had scraped the smooth surface of a table. After the gastronomic experience, the steer's long tongues were often sent on some personal exploration deep inside their wide nostrils.

Between each corral, a huge cement bathtub served as the main watering hole for the hundreds of thirsty animals. With the heat index reaching over 100 degrees, it was critical to have water at all times. The cemented watering containers used the same type of mechanical systems as most modern toilets. A long, hollow metal balloon floated on the surface of the water. When the thirsty cattle had downed the water levels, the mechanical tin floater signaled to leverage the need for the flow of more water. The water supply to the corrals came from two large, man-made reservoirs situated at the far north end of the feedlot. An assortment of birds, ducks, and fish could always be found in or near the moving water, which was tranquil only when the pump motors paused in their continu-ous efforts to fill the watering holes. All of God's winged creatures living nearby used the cement water holes in the corrals. A good relationship existed between the steers and the birds. Clearly, an "I need you" relationship was evident between the feedlot animals.

About twice a year, a great stink took place, as mammoth-size tractors with pushed the steer dung into piles of manure within the same corrals. The manure was hauled off to some unknown location. Just before the dung was piled, the floor of the corrals thickened, as if layers of floor had been added to the foundation. The penetrating stink stuck around for a while. It is funny now to think that it probably stunk all the time, but we became accustomed to the smell, unas-sumingly taking it for granted. It never failed that whenever we had relatives from the city or other parts of the state visit our home, they often signaled the strong stench of dry manure by tightly pinching their noses and holding their breath in front of us. Suddenly, they would explode with loud laughter adding smirked comment about our deteriorating living conditions. I presume that the men and women who work with cattle will always have a distinct smell that they take for granted, too.

Across the lot from the mill and corrals, an intriguing maze of steel formed smaller holding pens that led the cattle down narrow tunnels to boarding platforms where they embarked on their last journey to the slaughterhouses in Los Angeles. Hundreds of fattened steers with a mortified and stricken look in their eyes were herded into the motorized trailer for the long haul. Their heavy bodies, burdened with the scary anticipation of their fate, moved slowly into the boxed truck. Unfortunately, in these days, Los Angeles was the closest location to the Imperial Valley for processing beef.

During the calm times at the feedlot, the labyrinth of the steel chutes looked like California ghost towns after the gold rush. Of all the places on the feedlot, this was my favorite hiding place. I often wished I could view this area from fifty feet up. I was sure that I could discover additional nooks and crannies in the maze of steel.

Large sheets of metal firmly joined formed the maze of the corral chute. The metal sheets had a punched-out pattern of holes from top to bottom. The cookie-like patterns allowed air to flow in and out. The lower holes had marks and stains of dung and dried mud on the edges of sharp cut metal. The cattle were rushed from the corrals through these chutes until they ended up in the crowded semi-truck for the trip to the slaughter house. The unsettling effects of the cattle's tight quarters were noticeable during every trip. The middle and top holes on the metal chute showed signs of the unintended pushing and shoving from the steers. Traces of hair and blood could be spotted every-where too. A writer could easily formulate a detective story by just studying the remnants, stains and other evidence of the cattle.

The Saturday after, truckloads of new, young cattle arrived from the Lone Star State; we participated in branding them, injecting them with medicines, and cutting their tails and horns.

The cowboys were always sympathetic of the long ride the young steers had endured all the way from the cattle regions in Amarillo, Texas.   As a matter of fact, some of the cattle arrived sick or dead from the long trip or from being trampled by the others. After the welcoming routine, the young steers were placed in holding pens for a short while to monitor their health, then moved to the regular corrals to fatten up before we saw them next at the local grocery store.

The Rocking Arrow feedlot brand was an arrow pointing up from a half-moon base, resembling the pedestal of a rocking chair. The modern way of branding was so much different from what we had seen in México. At the Rocking Arrow, each of the newly arrived steers was forced to run though a chute to get to the large, electric holding machine, where thick, iron round spokes squeezed the animal mercilessly into place. The air-compressed machine could be heard from a distance, while the sound of the moaning steer painfully spilled from the hold. Cowboys stationed on both sides of the machine had just a few seconds to accomplish their initiation and inspection tasks. There was something inexplicable about the welcoming rituals of the cattle to the Rocking Arrow Ranch.

One man chopped the bushy part of the tail from the steer while another branded its hip. At the same time, another man cut off the sharp ends of the horns with huge clippers. Horn ends and bits bounced from the ground as the prominent smell of raw bone and burnt hair lingered over the entire process. My oldest brother stood at the front end of the line. His job was to stick a large metal stem far enough into the esophagus of the steer so that a large pill could be pushed forward, close to the first stomach of the animal. Meanwhile, another cowboy clipped an identification tag onto the animal's hairy ear. Each steer handled the process differently, but most were reluctant to move forward through the chutes. Because I was still so much smaller than even the youngest steers, my job was to stand outside the chutes and prod the cattle with a long tube that delivered a slight current of electric shock. The enthusiastic whistling, whooping and hollering of the cowboys, along with the prodding, gave the cattle the incentive to move along rather quickly and obediently through the steel chutes. From my position, I was able to see the animals as they went in whole and came out with their horns shooting streams of blood all over the corrals and sometimes on the clothes worn by the men. By the end of the day, a large pile of steer horns, tails, and skin remained as evidence of the unforgettable welcoming and initiation process. And not long after this, the cattle traveled again through the same chutes into the waiting trucks headed for the slaughterhouse. Speed was an important part of feedlot life.

The sounds of the feedlot varied, depending on the time of day. Loud cries, of course, were heard during the pushing and shoving of the loading and unloading of new cattle and during the branding process. But in the morning when the steers were hungry, they tilted their heads toward heaven and let out a pleading howl. On the rare cold mornings, the group of steers looked like smoking chimneys in the Midwest during the wintry days. Clouds of hot, bad breath floated out of their mouths and noses, mixing with the chilly air. I once thought that perhaps they, too, had their God, and the morning ritual was an offering of sorts and snorts.

The special sounds of the Redwing black birds harmonized well with the bellowing steers, creating a unique symphony of feedlot sounds from early morning to dusk. The birds were crazy about the seeds that dropped from the feed truck and from the silage bins. They also enjoyed the many buzzing insects effortlessly flying close to the cattle. The birds often sat on the backs of the fat steers, waiting for the bugs and insects that danced a few inches from the cattle.

Redwing blackbirds were the most common birds at the feedlot. Many white-tipped doves were also competing for the open spaces with rich deposits of scattered grain. But my favorite bird was a tiny, gray swallow that nested beneath the wooden shades in the corrals. Their nests were not easy to reach, but I devised a method. I jumped into the corrals and pretended that I knew what I was doing, being so close to the huge steers, who continued to chew and chew. Most of the oversized steers paid no attention to me, but the wiser ones seemed to stare with great regard, as I crossed their paths to reach the birds. I always felt safe when I reached the cemented poles. First, I jumped onto the cement base of the iron poles that held up the shades, covering my arms and legs with a yellowish, powdery dust of rust. With my legs wrapped around the four-inch-diameter pole, I reached as high as possible and scooted my way up until I reached the point where the iron pole and the shade formed a right angle. Just as my mother liked to build altars in the corner, the birds also built nests under the corner where the shade and pole met. The nest was protected from the glaring desert sun and stifling summer heat. By hanging onto the pole with my left arm and hand, I could ease my right hand into the nest.

If I felt the delicate warm shells of the eggs, I left the nest alone at once. But if my fingers felt a warm and fuzzy bundle, I knew the babies had recently hatched, and I pulled them out of the nest and held them in my hand to study them. I was fascinated by their behavior and amazed at their quick development. Some hatchlings stretched their necks too far out of the nest in search of food and fell into the soft manure twelve feet below. Those birds I took home to care for under a warm lamp in the bedroom my sister and I shared. There was always something growing in our room, ranging from baby birds under the homemade lamp incubator to baby mice born under our beds; neither bothered us.

With the presence of many winged animals, cats were abundant too. This was the first time I had seen so many cats in one place, at one time. They not only had the delectable meals of fowl and feathers available, they also had the chasing feasts of mice, if they so desired. The cats in the ranch were given preferential treatment by the office employees, who fed them stinky food from small cans. The canned food for the cats was a new custom for us coming from México. The only tin cans we were familiar with were filled with lard, sugar and other human foods. We had no idea that food was packed so nicely for cats. Most surprising was that the cats were spoiled to the point of laziness. Their energetic appetite for chasing mice or surprising birds was taken from them. Many of the cats became fat and complacent, waiting for the arrival of the men who would feed them.

At the Rocking Arrow Ranch, beef meals were abundant. The occasional, unlucky steer was permanently damaged if a leg was broken when their hoofs were caught and tangled during the boarding process. The truck would not take injured animals to the slaughterhouse. The cattle tripped over each other, and their fat, swollen bodies were not capable of managing in the same manner as when they were skinny. The cowhands soon put the steer out of its misery, and then all the men pitched in to skin, cut, clean, and package the meat for the workers' families to eat.

My mother made a name for herself around the ranch with her fantastic cooking skills. It all started one Saturday when she sent me to the feedlot mill with pork meat burritos made with fresh flour tortillas for my father's morning snack. On one occasion, he shared his mid-day snack with one of his bosses, who praised my mother's cooking and bragged about this to the others. Soon after, they could not get enough of her burritos. About twice a month on Saturdays, until the day we left the ranch in 1968, my mother sent me to the ranch with a paper sack filled with burritos for my father's bosses. It seemed to me that the burrito sack got bigger as the years passed. For my father, it was a way to show his bosses how much our family appreciated all the help they had given us in our new homeland. The burritos were a way to ingratiate ourselves with those that had helped my father by providing him a stable job and a decent way to keep the family together.

The trips to the ranch gave me the opportunity to learn more about the people with whom my father worked at the feedlot. Being the youngest, I was able to freely mingle with my father and his coworkers in a male-dominated culture. He also took me on the big feed truck for rides, up and down the corral aisles. He drove with his head stuck out the driver's window in order to monitor the amount of food the truck was spilling through a thick, leathery spout protruding from behind the cabin. The smell of the freshly-mixed silage was as soothing to me as hot tea on a cold day. I thought my father was the greatest driver in the world. He also made 50,000 hungry head of cattle extremely happy.

By the time I was ten, my only dream was to become a cowgirl. I learned to brand and cut steer tails and horns. I knew how to saddle and ride uneasy horses. I dreamed of injecting the cattle and caring for the sick ones. I also learned how to soften leather for the horse saddles and cowboy ropes. I really enjoyed the opportunity to survey the feedlot on horseback. Identifying sickly steers was the responsibility of the cowhand. Learning to operate the enormous engines of the mill and mixing the proper ingredients for the cattle was a great prospective career. I truly enjoyed the outdoors of the feedlot, along with the birds and cattle.

The bookkeeper at the feedlot knew of my childhood dreams, and with my limited English I proudly told him about my future adventures as a cowgirl. One summer day, *El Pecoso*, feedlot accountant for the Rocking Arrow Ranch, asked me to place my foot on a sheet of blank paper. With a pencil, he carefully sketched around the edges of my foot. I guessed that he was measuring my foot for the hand-me-down shoes that we received in boxes about twice a year. We were always surprised with "gently worn" clothes and shoes from the daughters and relatives of the men working the business side of the feedlot. But a few weeks later, *El Pecoso* handed me a large square box, containing a pair of red cowgirl boots. This was the greatest present I had ever received! I had never seen such large shoe boxes in my life. The red cowboy boots were so beautiful: my second present from an American. I felt my heart jumping at the sight of these fancy red boots, fitted especially for my new career. Flashes of branding and horse riding in my new boots raced through my mind.

Immediately, the men wanted me to wear the beautiful boots. All along, they knew that I was an impressionable young girl. I quickly but politely removed my tennis shoes and stuck my foot into one of the boots. Everyone was intently watching every moment. Then I stuck the other foot into the second boot. The four or five men watching seem to be enjoying the moment with me. I finally stood in with both feet inside the sturdy leather boots. What would I say to my mother and father? I began to think. My parents would think that I asked for the boots. Asking Americans for things was not an acceptable behavior in our family. We were strictly advised and directed to not be trouble for the *Americanos*. We were required to be on our best behavior at all times no matter what circumstances were facing us.

As soon as my entire weight was in the beautiful red boots, I could feel a pinching, which I did not mention. I shared my thanks and appreciation and promised more of my mother's delicious pork burritos. I knew that I had to convince my mother to cook more pork burritos for the next time. I was so appreciative that I made it a point to help make more of my mother's burritos. But I did not say much else.

Unfortunately, the boots were too tight for my growing feet, and wearing them only disappointed me with the pain. I wanted to say something to *El Pecoso*, but my mother did not want me to create any problems in our new community. After all, our entire family depended on the feedlot. I never said a word about the boots and only wore them once; they were later handed down to my niece, María. To this day I regret not having the courage to say anything about the boots that could have been easily exchanged for a larger size. We were trying hard to be welcomed to this country and, therefore, we kept many of our emotions and feelings to ourselves. In my early days in California, I did not like the fact that I could not join the Girl Scouts or the church youth group because we lived so far away from town. In the family, the cars were for working people and not for driving children to their activities. School buses were the only transportation in and out of our country home, except for the weekly trip to purchase groceries. But in the long run, I never regretted living in the isolated environment of the desert ranch. The Rocking Arrow served as a living American classroom unlike any other.

Living surrounded by irrigated alfalfa fields under the beautiful, wispy clouds and, at a short distance the light dust from the cattle rising like a mirage, in many ways added much color to early learning. Living in a remote area with minimal interference or interruptions from neighbors or loud cars gave many wonderful opportunities for family conversations. By the time we gathered for dinner, the noisy mill in the distance was resting from its full day of grinding and churning cow feed.

The rural Imperial Valley environment prevented us from growing up too fast, too soon, and instead provided the needed time to slowly mature into our new homeland within the limitations of our meager budgets. Life did not rush through without teaching us important and valuable lessons of work, friendship and family. The Rocking Arrow days embedded in our family a special bond and unity unique to growing up in the rural environment.

Mouse Trap

1965

Myra Ford became my good friend in the early 1960s. She was the daughter of Denny Ford, better known as "*El Deny*," the foreman at the feedlot where my father tended the fifteen thousand head of cattle. One day, *El Deny* told my father that he had a daughter about my age and that he could bring her to play with me. My father thought this was great news — a sign of acceptance of our family. I could serve as a bridge between two cultures and two families in our early days in the United States. My father always wanted to please his bosses, and this was truly one strong message of support.

Looking back, I assume many people thought we had little to do out in the country or that we might have been bored living in the middle of alfalfa and cotton fields. Many folks around us thought the country was boring. Perhaps this was one of several reasons Mr. Ford was motivated to introduce Myra to my family and me. Myra visited on a Saturday morning. Denny told my father that he was going to drop her off at our house so that we could play together. The anticipation of Myra's visit was a mixture of excitement and concern. We were, after all, expected to be pleasant and accommodating to my father's bosses and their children. If we failed to be gracious, we were sure our father would hear of this or that.

I remember taking a bath the Friday night before Myra's visit. I wanted to please, and my parents wanted to make sure that I welcomed Myra as a special friend. I also remember that my mother gave us all instructions on house cleaning and manners, even though my brothers would not see Myra arrive because they were going to be at work. At lunchtime, though, Myra joined all of us at the kitchen table.

Around ten o'clock that special Saturday morning, Mr. Ford left the feedlot and drove to the small neighboring town of Calipatria. From the kitchen window we could see his white '62 Ford pickup leaving at this unusual time from work. My mother and I knew that meant Myra would soon arrive. We had seen her before from a distance; she was a pretty girl with blond hair. I knew she was about my age and size, because her father often brought us some of her unwanted clothes, neatly folded in a cardboard box.

Soon Mr. Ford stopped his dusty pickup on the main dirt-and-gravel road, about forty feet away from our house. My heart pounded with delight at the prospect of having a new playmate. Myra waited for her father to come around to the passenger side

of the white work truck and open her door. The first things I saw
were her long legs jumping down to the ground. We watched
through the small kitchen window until Myra started toward the
house. My mother encouraged me to welcome our guests to our
home, and I quickly left through the back door to greet them.

Two large salt cedars near the house served as nature's welcome
mat for visitors. I could feel their shadows follow me past the small
ditch and onto the wooden bridge over the irrigation canal that
divided the house from the main road. To my surprise, Myra's dad
was unloading two bikes and several mysterious bags, truly a great
surprise. This was one of the few times in my childhood when I
was aware that my siblings and I did not have much material
wealth compared to other children our age.

Mr. Ford, a handsome, strong man in his late forties, greeted me
with a friendly "Hi, there." I knew him already, thanks to my
mother's pork burritos that were so popular with all the Rocking
Arrow men. He was one of the most gracious men at the feedlot.
He introduced his daughter to me and handed me a brown paper
bag to carry. He parked the bikes just a few feet away from the
road next to the canal. Then he said goodbye to Myra, got back in
his pickup, and left us in a dusty cloud of powdery dirt. Myra and I
smiled at each other as her father sped away toward the feedlot.
My English must have been good enough, because we hit it off and
were friends from then on.

During Myra's brief visit that day, we rode bikes and played with

the games she had brought with her. I remember playing Mouse
Trap and Monopoly for the first time ever. The Mouse Trap game
was my favorite. Myra showed me how to toss the dice for my
turn and how to move the mouse along the colorful playing board
before it was caught in a simple contraption designed to entertain
us. Everyone watched with anticipation as the plastic trap finally
fell over the mouse, determining the winners and losers of the
game. At the end of the game, the winners were always cheering
and clapping with much excitement!

*I wish that I had games like those of Myra. How lucky she must
be to have so many things*, I thought. She had it all. I really did not
have many playthings — just an old set of paper dolls that my
sister and I bought for ninety-nine cents.

Fortunately, my father had made some valuable suggestions to me
about entertaining my new friend. On his recommendations, I
showed Myra the baby pinto kittens that had been born under the
house. The mother cat was still feeding the babies and waiting for
their eyes to open. As always, I had to push myself through a small
opening halfway into the crawl space of the house in order to pull
out one of the tiny, yellow kittens. Myra really liked that part of her
visit.

I took her to my hideout at the top of a salt cedar. From the
summit of the fruitless tree, we could see the Rocking Arrow and
the roof of the house. I also showed Myra our reservoir filled with
water and the small ditch that brought the water from the main

canal. The ditches were used for irrigation of all the growing crops around us. From the reservoir's banks, we could see the hundreds of minnows swimming away from the center current. I showed her how I spent many hours of my day catching the tiny fish and feeding them to the hungry cats. I could tell that these experiences were new to Myra. Finally, I presented my bird nests and the empty eggshells I collected from local birds. I do not remember whether Myra liked what I showed her, but it must have been different from the kind of things she had at home.

Not long after, my father brought me a printed invitation to Myra's birthday party — the first such party I have had asked to attend in our new country; it was a nice invitation, with my name specifically written on it by Myra. In our small village in México, no one ever could afford to print paper invitations with fancy words or colorful designs. If a party took place, no one was excluded; everyone knew about it and was welcome to attend. I thought that the Fords had to be rich to spend their money on a party just for one occasion. In our family and with limited resources, one party was planned for celebrating many occasions at once. The young and the old were always the most celebrated during our family gatherings.

Myra's party was an awesome event for me. First, we were treated to Mexican food about fifty miles from home. A dozen of us sat around the restaurant table ordering tacos, enchiladas, and chimichangas. For the first time, I heard non-Spanish-speaking children ordering Mexican food in what sounded like a much different dialect of Spanish than my own. Nobody bothered with the correct pronunciation of tacos and enchiladas, but I did not say a word about this to anyone. I worried instead what they thought of my English. I am certain that I was not capable of pronouncing some English words properly and must have had a heavy accent for most, if not all, of my American vocabulary.

After the meal, we were taken by car to a nearby roller skating rink; I had never seen such a thing before. The large building offer a cozy environment for the roller rink. Loud music played as children roller skated round and round. I watched in amazement, noting what everyone else did before making any move of my own. Myra had her own skates, but most of the rest of us were escorted to the counter to rent skates fit for our size. For me, this was another hurdle. I did not know what size I wore. Most of the shoes we wore were given to us or bought at the stores after trying the approximate size.

When my family needed shoes, we bought them at the five-and-ten-cent stores, where we searched for the right size by trying on various pairs from a pile of the same style stacked high in a bin. But all the other children at the party knew their shoe size. I looked at my shoes and quickly surveyed the feet of the other girls. Myra's feet were bigger than mine, so I pointed to Andrea, soliciting the same-size skates. Andrea's feet were also bigger than mine, but I never complained about the extra space between my toes and the tip of the skates.

The leather boots and wooden wheels attached to the skates felt clumsy. Although I had athletic skill and good balance, my abilities on the rink were nothing compared to Myra's and the other children's. It was apparent that this was not their first time visiting the skating rink. I hung on the side rail and dragged myself until I felt sure of the wheels under my feet, then pushed off for a few seconds, gliding on the slippery wood rink until my inexperienced legs began to go in opposite directions. Myra and her friends seemed to be roller skating past me at breakneck speed.

A few days after the birthday party, Mr. Ford brought me a gift from Myra. She had received duplicate board games for her birthday and was willing to share one with me. Now I had my own colorful Mouse Trap board game! The box alone was impressive to a child's eyes. When my mother saw the beautiful glossy Mouse Trap box, her eyes and her smile met mine with a sense of approval. At that time, it would have been unreasonable for my parents to spend their money on children's games. We all knew that my father could barely feed us, let alone buy us such games.

Some time after that, I was invited to Myra's home in Calipatria. It was a pretty, tidy house, carpeted and air-conditioned and across from a city park. Her mother, the local postmaster, was kind to me. For lunch, she fixed sweet sandwiches, which turned out to be peanut butter and jelly. When we played games in the afternoon, I noticed their house was not as noisy as ours. Only three people lived at Myra's home, compared to our seven or sometimes more, and her house had a quiet air-conditioner. In contrast, our water coolers resembled crop dusters flying only inches above the floor, blowing air and making a lot of unnecessary noise. It was the best we had. During the hot summer months, our desert home rattled at all hours, as the coolers huffed and puffed across the watered sheets of dried yellow grass. I thought Myra had a nicer home. In my family, we all thought that Myra and her parents were wealthy.

Perhaps the most interesting part of my visit to Myra's was seeing her pet skunk that at first shocked me. The only skunks I was used to seeing were the ones that crossed the road and lifted their tails to spray anyone who came too close, and also, of course, the ones smashed like blue corn tortillas on the road. My father told us that the skunk spray could blind us, so we stayed far away when we saw one. They smelled so bad. We usually knew when one was within a mile of us. But Myra's skunk was sitting on the sofa the first time I saw it. Myra's mother told me not to be afraid of this skunk because it was a nice one; it did smell nice. I believe the animal doctor had something to do with the removal the animal's stink glands. Life in the United States was full of new wonders.

My friendship with Myra provided me with many "firsts" and opportunities, as my family and I integrated into a new life with a foreign twist. Myra and her family provided an important balance that served me well later in life. Our success and spirit is due in part thanks to the kindness and welcoming attitudes we received from people like the Fords who were willing to include us as part of their circle of friends!

Merry Christmas, Little Sister!

1966

During the Christmas holidays, we celebrated like many Catholic families in the United States in the 1960s. We attended the packed midnight mass and ate many different festive foods, including *tamales*, *buñuelos* (fried tortillas resembling elephant ears) and *atole* (a sweet drink made with corn meal). The house was decorated with a religious *nacimiento* (nativity scene) for the *Navidad* (Christmas) and a skimpy mountain pine tree. My mother made all of the tiny cardboard houses that rested on the painted green hills of the *nacimiento*. The miniature lighted scene set the tone for a festive holiday mood in our country home.

Cherished Mexican Christmas traditions were mingled with American ones. At the time, we did not know that even America had borrowed Christmas traditions from other immigrant groups before us, including that of the indoor decorated Christmas tree. My fourth grade teacher made sure that we knew it was the

Germans who introduced the tradition of decorating Christmas trees. She was a first generation German-American. At first we chuckled at the idea of a tree inside the house, but once it was decorated, we admired the unfamiliar beauty and wondered why Mexicans did not have the idea first. Under the tree were neatly wrapped presents my mother had painstakingly assembled, while we children were at school. The smells in our house, however, were purely Mexican following the family *tamalada* (making and eating tamales).

We were all too familiar with the odor of steamed corn husks signaling the time to remove the fresh tamales from the hot stove. My mother labored to keep the old customs in place, even when the new ones became more enticing and also part of our American home life.

Christmas at school was very different too. In early grades, we were escorted to the school cafeteria to meet the jolly man with the white beard and mustache. The velveteen suited man did not speak Spanish, and therefore, we did not understand a word he said. He handed out brown bags filled with peanuts, candy, an apple and an orange. Some years, the bags also contained popcorn. Year after year, the brown bag filled with simple goodies was taken home to share with the family. Other times, we traded small gifts with secret pals in our classrooms.

Our curiosity about Christmas in the United States was also fueled by my father's English-speaking employers. The

Rocking Arrow feedlot celebrated Christmas in many ways, which helped to teach us things about the holiday that, otherwise, would have taken years to fully understand.

My father worked seven days a week feeding the fifty thousand head of cattle at Rocking Arrow. As a young girl excited about Christmas, it seemed to me that even the cows were in the holiday spirit! My father's bosses were cattlemen from Amarillo, Texas, and had hearts as big as their native state, when it came to the Zendejas family. During the holidays, they brought us boxes of clothes that their families no longer wanted. We danced for joy, anxious to open the cardboard boxes of fancy, second-hand American outfits in some cases requiring some alterations before wearing. We always relished the leftover delicacies from their festive Christmas parties.

Every day except Saturday, we cleaned the feedlot office. During the holiday season, chocolate candies were abundant in fancy boxes, and we could hardly wait to pop open the boxes inscribed with lacy black writing. Every piece of candy rested in its own skirt of fancy paper. Some candies were even wrapped in colorful foil paper nestled inside a ruffled basket. We tried to make the gaps we left inside the boxes as inconspicuous as possible, as we had been instructed not to take anything from these important, cigar-smelling rooms.

The trash cans at the feedlot offices were holiday treasure-troves. We found unopened mailing cardboard tubes with calendars picturing women in skimpy lingerie sitting on Santa's lap. Often, Christmas calendar gifts sent to the feedlot from other businesses were just thrown in the trash. With all these surprises waiting for us, Christmas was definitely the best time of year to be in the cleaning business.

In 1964, the holiday season began for me when a large and fancy wrapped box appeared under the meager Christmas tree. That big package was for me, and everyone in the family made sure I knew it was there. My brothers and sister bragged that the biggest present under the tree belonged to me. I was truly absorbed by this enormous gift. Everyone, including my father and mother, joined in the excitement over the unusually large present. Although we did get bikes one Christmas, most of the gifts we received were smaller packages containing clothes for school or plastic dolls.

Never before had I been as excited about the American Christmas as I was this particular festive year. The more my family spoke of the possible contents in the box, the more excited I became, antici-pating a beautiful new bike or a wooden doll house. While we lived comfortably, by today's standards we were poor, so the prospect of such a big gift preoccupied my thinking.

My brother Alfonso was head cheerleader, when it came to the enormous, wrapped box. His charismatic smile and laughter were contagious. His infectious and entertaining personality covered up his well- planned, outlandish scheme. All he needed were

Texas-sized Longhorn pompoms to complete the props of this plot. If anyone in the family could spur excitement and chatter over inconsequential things, it was Alfonso. The entire family chatted about the mysterious gift; at the time, no one mentioned who had brought it or who had wrapped it. The carefully wrapped present just sat there, lending itself to a joyous discussion every night before Christmas Eve.

In México, the traditional gift-giving took place on January 6, *El Día De Los Reyes Magos* (Day of the Wise Men). My mother told us that this was the day the Wise Men arrived at the manger with the gifts for baby Jesus. In México, gifts are also only for the children. We placed our shoes squarely by the door on January 5 and woke up early to see what the Three Kings had left for us. I remember telling everyone on this occasion that I liked Santa Claus and Christmas Eve better, because the big box could not possibly fit in my tattered Mexican shoes.

At long last, Christmas Eve arrived, and the whole day seemed filled with mystery. My anxiety amplified as the big night approached. While we prayed the rosary and chanted traditional Mexican religious holiday songs, my heart raced hours ahead, imagining the greatest present that I would ever receive. Best of all, it was from my family. As the youngest, I enjoyed some favors; yet this surprise was a true privilege I had not anticipated. But first, as was our new yearly custom, we would drive five miles away to our local church before returning home to eat the festive holiday meal. After supper, we would gather to form our own procession, parading the plaster figures of Mary and Joseph on a platform of cardboard and plywood. My mother and father might invite their few new friends to join us. I went over and over these preliminary events in my mind, eager for the moment when at last I could open the gigantic gift.

After mass, we sat on the vinyl kitchen chairs or on the small single bed in the far corner of the living room. I remember sitting on the linoleum floor, as it seemed the appropriate place to handle the large and interesting box. Everyone was ready to open gifts, and everyone was eager for me to open mine. The smaller gifts were passed around, and the noise of the wrapping paper being shredded away drowned out our murmurs of appreciation. Finally, Alfonso placed the big box in front of my knees. His big smile, high cheekbones, and rosy complexion made him perfect for the role of Santa.

By this time, the anticipation had created a lathering of my enthused emotions. The box was festively wrapped and looked large enough to hold nine boxes of ladies' shoes. When I reached to move the box closer, I could tell it was not a heavy present, which made me even more curious.

Carefully, I broke the shiny ribbon and tore the paper from the top of the box. I opened the cardboard flaps, noting that the printing referred to the box's original contents, so this was not a present I could identify by the carton. Behind the cardboard flaps, I could see a smaller box inside the first one. I glanced around at my family, and their bright smiles encouraged me to hurry up. I pulled open the flaps of the smaller box to find my gift.

My excitement changed to discomfort as my eyes and nose coordinated efforts to define the contents. A sharp dagger went through my 10-year-old heart. I wanted to cry, but everyone else was laughing. I wanted to scream while everyone was pointing and holding their bellies. Inside the box were two neatly arranged piles of dried cow chips, all about the same size, three to a pile. The smell of manure was overwhelming. I pushed the box aside with a frown of disapproval. I could feel my mother's small, dark-brown eyes send warmth to me in the middle of this childhood tragedy. It was my father's and mother's love that helped me endure this short-lived but memorable event for the entire family.

To this date, the family story of the cow chip Christmas present is repeated at every gathering and generates the same boisterous laughter that I remember from more than thirty-five years ago. Now, as the story is told over and over again, the nephews and nieces laugh along with the fathers and mothers.

This childhood experience could have damaged my self-esteem or could have caused social ramifications or behavior problems. But the fact of the matter is that the love of my family was so much greater than this one experience that I did not have much room to feel sorry for myself. We were taught never to feel sorry for the humble life, honest work or humble food on our table.

As the youngest of the family, I knew that the cow chip *Feliz Navidad* (Merry Christmas) present was just my big brother teasing me as usual. I should have known better, since we really did not have money to purchase large-type gifts for anyone in the family. Truly, this lesson has been an unforgettable and life-long one. I realized then not to expect gifts of value from others, but to work hard and earn my own rewards. I realized that it was so much more important to give than to receive.

Silk Curtains

1964

Our first home in California was out of the way of major paved roads and city lights. We lived in the stillness of the rural county, smack in the path of the beautiful, picturesque sunsets of the California desert. Our borrowed home, a plain cement-block house, had windows on all four sides, offering us a variety of scenic country views.

At sundown, a glistening ribbon of the distant Salton Sea could be seen from any elevated area around the home and from the roof. From my parents' room and the kitchen windows, the view was of the dirt road arriving from the west. The bathroom windows opened to a view of the alfalfa field or whatever else was planted to the south at different times of the year. As the common eye would suspect, the brightest rooms were on the east and west of the house. It was obvious that maintaining a comfortable temperature was never a design concern, since the kitchen window hosted the scorching heat from the hot sun. Large tin box coolers, which fit through the upper panes of the windows, helped to keep the inside temper-ature tolerable. It seemed to me that whenever the straw-like mats below the cooler panels were watered, fresh, cool streams of air blew inside the home.

The south windows in our room provided a softer view of the desert terrain of the mountains. Alfalfa fields, green all year round, extended as far as the eye could see; gazing at them had a special, calming effect on me. To the north and east of the house, the vista was interrupted by the huge salt cedars that grew along the irrigation canal. The giant trees provided much-needed shade and housed the many birds, whose pretty songs I enjoyed.

When we first moved in, my mother adopted whatever was left on the windows. Soon after, dime-store cheap curtains dressed the humble home. Then, a year or so later my mother was given someone's discarded white parachute. At the first sight of the huge ball of material, my mother's immediate plan of action was formed. When my mother had an idea, she made sure it was realized. She was set in her mind that our home was going to have real silk curtains.

My mother spent many hours cutting, sewing, and arranging the new curtains. The light, silky material hung in every room of the house, including the kitchen. She was proud of her new, homemade curtains. I was probably the only one in the family who noticed the thick lines of parachute thread that crisscrossed the material.

One lazy Saturday afternoon when I was ten, I took out a pair of scissors to cut and sew doll outfits, my favorite indoor pastime. As I sat by my parent's bedroom window cutting material, I decided to use a tiny piece from the bottom of the silk curtain hanging next to me. *No one will notice*, I thought.

The feeling of cutting silky rayon with scissors is rewarding to the senses, and the smoothness of the material makes it so simple to do. I spread the long blades of the scissors and cut a long, uneven path. It was hypnotizing. I cut through almost the entire lower half of my mother's curtain.

When I realized what I had done, I tried to hide the damage. I pulled the pieces of the curtain together and moved a chair in front to hold the mess together.

But, of course, my mother quickly noticed the changes in her bedroom, including the torn pieces at the bottom of the silk. The parachute had survived many training jumps from hundreds of feet above sea level but had not escaped the hands of a mischievous child.

My mother was furious. She had spent so many hours trying to make our home look nice, cautiously measuring the height and width of every window to make sure she cut the silk at just the right length. She spent many hours peddling the sewing machine into action. To find one of her curtains destroyed was more than she could bear.

Her determined voice called for all of us —Hector, Blanca, Luis, and I— to stand in front of her while she lectured us about this intolerable crime. She felt like a victim and wanted to know who was responsible. No one said a thing, and then — I do not know why — I opened my unsympathetic mouth.

"I think Luis did it," I said softly in Spanish. All unpleasant eyes turned toward Luis. He was the least likely to do something like this. He was the quietest and never bragged about anything. He protested his innocence, pleading with my mother. He rarely showed any emotion, so his tears were so credible they convinced my mother that he was not guilty. She again surveyed the remaining three of us. My mother immediately made an accurate and decisive assessment of the current situation.

Everyone stood at attention. The question was: If Luis did not do it, then who did? Hector and Blanca pointed at me and called out my name, accusing me of cutting the pretty curtains. "Espy did it," they yelped simultaneously.

The serious attention turned to me, and tears began to well up in my eyes. I was the one who had cut up the silky curtains. I was the one who had pointed to Luis as the responsible one. I knew I would be punished, but my tears poured down my cheeks from a sense of relief. The case was solved.

I was guilty and could not hide the truth. The only safe place for me to hide was next to my father, but he was still at work. I rushed to the curtain-covered closet, where I sometimes hid, until he arrived to defend me from the grown children. I always knew that I would have my father's sympathy. But I knew I had lost some of my integrity.

My mother made sure everyone went back to doing whatever it was they had been doing, then dragged me from the closet and scolded me as never before. Her anger was not so much about the curtain being torn up, but more so, it was about my not accepting the blame for something I had done. In her gentle but firm manner, she made me understand the importance of acknowledging my own actions, no matter how difficult.

My mother taught me a lesson by having me sew the curtain back together. The white silk parachute curtains lasted us until we moved in 1968. Until then, the extra line of thread on the one curtain served as a constant reminder of my devious action.

Like other family stories, the parachute curtain incident has been retold many times. If there are lessons to be learned, this one is a classic. The retelling always makes me feel bad about my behavior, and I promised again to myself never to blame anyone else for something I did. In the long run, telling the truth is less of a burden on the soul. A parachute helped me early in my life to learn a difficult lesson, which landed softly on the support and love of my mother.

An Accident

1963

J ust as the East Coast has its seasons, our home also had its
seasons. The farming of wheat, cotton, alfalfa and vegetables painted the ground in different colors ranging from
Amazon green to mustard yellow. In late fall, the spotted white
balls of cotton on the drying plant signaled a cooler season for the
speedy desert roadrunner. In the midst of the cotton fields, the
dried cotton blossoms, so tender and so white, decorated the
landscape for the coming of the holidays.

When the Imperial Valley sun decided that it had filtered enough
heat to our desert environment, the colors again changed. In late
spring and early summer, the freshly-cut green alfalfa fields deo-
dorized and freshened the dusty desert, spreading a pleasant green
air scent in our environment, an unforgettable smell for us.
During the summer, the flowing blades of tall green grasses
softened the blow of the immense heat on our childhood faces.

Another unforgettable sight and sound was the early wake-up calls of the propelled crop duster painted in colors resembling a fierce yellow-jacket. The single-seat, noisy plane spluttered sounds as it took off and landed next to our home. The straight and flat border of a waste-water canal served as the runway. The fascinating flying machine left its white plumes of chemicals lined from one end of the green fields to the other. The only other airplanes we had encountered were the ones that flew high over our Mexican village skies. Men in sombreros and women in *rebosos* (shawls) turned their heads at the barely-audible sound to catch a glimpse of the airplane as the *avión* (airplane) crossed high in the heavens over our village.

Our humble home was located within a few yards of the intricate waterways. It was one of the canals, Lateral M to be exact, that introduced me to the world of irrigation and to an early understanding of the cycles of life.

My father could not have chosen a more perfect place for us to live after we immigrated to the United States. I know that my father was often encouraged by others to move the family to more appropriate location's where jobs for all were plentiful. Most of our relatives had moved to the thriving cities in the States. My father would not hear of moving anywhere else, but remained in the Imperial Valley feeding his thousands of cattle and his family.

Soon after arriving in California, we all learned the rules and expectations of our new home. We enjoyed a completely different

freedom in our California home, as compared to our life in the
Mexican mountain village.

As a child, it seemed to me that we would live and die in the
Imperial Valley. On many occasions, the carcasses of dead
animals drying up in the desert sun made it simple to assume
that we, too, would someday be buried in the saltine clay of the
hardened, fossil ocean floor. It amazed me that tiny shells could
always be found resting on or near the decaying animals. Perhaps
some day, I, too, would be surrounded by these tiny shells found in
this strange desert.

In our family, we were taught to ask permission for just about
everything except going to the bathroom. I now know that it was
for our protection and not meant to overburden the growing-up
process. Our Catholic faith and beliefs also added to the layers
of expectations in the manner of doing things around the house.
Yet, as is the case for many young adults, many of the things we
longed for were forbidden in our home. Even the mere mention
of matters of discomfort brought sharp looks from all the members
of the family, especially mi *Amá y Apá* (we fondly shorten the
words "Mamá" and "Papá"). Because of our gender and culture,
my sister and I were expected to keep our mother informed of
every move we made outside the home. Nothing less was expected.

My first encounter with the thought of dying came one sunny
afternoon along the canals of Imperial Valley. The day began like
most others, except on this day my brother Luis brought home a

borrowed toy. The sound of a noisy motorcycle approached our country home. Luis arrived riding into our yard on the borrowed cycle. We were too poor to afford machines that made such loud exhaust sounds. The only machines we owned were our used car and an old, roller-type washing machine that was given to us.

In his confident and convincing, sweet-talking voice, he invited me to hop on the back part of the seat. I glanced around for *mi Amá*, feeling a sense of premature guilt. I should have gone inside to ask permission to ride the fascinating machine, but I did not. It was a situation in which it seemed that my brother needed a "partner in crime."

Bracing one soft tennis shoe against the rear tire, I grabbed my brother's shoulder with my left hand and swung my right leg up and over the motorcycle seat, as if it were a horse. I wrapped my arms around my brother's waist, and off we went, flying along the country roads alongside the canals. A whiff of different country smells quickly passed through my nose. The smell of waste-water and freshly-cut plants was most common. The smell of dead fish and the sounds of water splashing also quickly came and went. The wonders of the wild desert wind smacked into our innocent and rural faces, as we sped forward in this adventure. We were so happy cutting through the warm wind, as if we were traveling at speeds unknown to man. We were happy, and for the moment, that was what counted.

Imperial Valley dirt roads are often dusty, due to limited rainfall and winds blowing sand onto the roadways. The motorcycle flirted with the dust, as we flew on two wheels through lingering smells and sounds. Luis steered the bike like a real pro, managing along the edge of one of the wastewater canals, the kind that carries dirty water full of fertilizer chemicals to the Salton Sea.

The motorcycle began to dance and skip in an unexpected patch of thick, loosened dirt. With no time to react, we lost our balance and were thrown from the bike. I landed softly on the canal's edge. My brother landed a few yards away. The bike was in a third location, with one spinning wheel reckoning toward us, as if snickering after our fall. No sounds of laughter or pain were heard. The stillness of the valley engulfed our emotions.

The motorcycle's motor was still running on its side and shaking the dust into the air, when we got up to shake the dust from our clothes with nervous hands. I do not remember crying; it would not have been the thing to do in front of my big brother. After all, he had invited me, and I had accepted. At an early age, we had learned to deal with consequences, and this was no exception for me. Besides, if I did show signs of weakness, Luis might not invite me on another well-deserved adventure. If I had acted like a small child over such an insignificant event, I would never have heard the end of it, either. In spirit, I acted tough and ready to go again. I was, however, a little scared. Luis asked if I was hurt. Though my body was shaking and my hands and legs were sore from the fall, I quickly jumped back on the bike behind him. I felt as if I had been thrown off a horse and no different.

I know that both our hearts were hotrods, racing as we headed back home. *Mi Amá* would be able to tell that we had fallen, as our clothes were loaded with stick dirt and our brown skin powdered with dust. I could not hide the dust in my eyebrows or lashes, let alone my long, light brown hair. There was no way to hide the accident or the clinging dirt. We knew we would be scolded for leaving without asking permission. Luis would be in trouble for taking me on the bike ride without any regard for our mother's approval. An unspoken mixture of emotions lingered over our heads as we approached our humble home. An antici-pated, bitter-sweet outcome awaited us.

We drove over the small canal located only a few hundred feet away from the house. The covered patio provided the only shade during the hot days. The thin strips of wood tied together with wire covered an area equivalent to a two-car garage. *Mi Apá's* feedlot bosses had been kind in allowing the building of the porch cover and providing the materials, which resembled the shade construction for the cattle. During our short motorcycle ride home, I could clearly see the six thin pipe poles holding the shades up about ten feet high. The shades created linear designs on the hard dirt.

Once off the bike and in the house, we got what we expected. The guilt our mother laid on us was worse than the fall itself. She reminded us that God would punish us for not listening to our parents. After the scolding, she inspected me from head to foot. I was still her baby, although ten at the time. My mother asked about our pains and sore spots, but my brother Luis was too humiliated to answer. I was not about to open my mouth. It was clear that my father would hear of this when he returned from work. When things like this happened, my mother usually did not say much or do anything until she and my father were alone. It was then that she told on us or defended us from any cones-quences *mi Apá* had to offer. My father usually shrugged off any ill feelings about the negative incidents in the family. He would surely chuckle at the thought of the small bike bucking us off and make some kind of statement that we were not smart enough to stay on the cycle, as he had thought. He would probably make a joke about how funny the scene must have been, as we rolled off the motorized bike, and laugh mockingly at our fall.

No one could deny that my left hand immediately began to swell. My mother escorted me to the bathroom to clean up, while she prepared her favorite remedy for swelling. At the same time, she had already begun the supper for the family. The smell of some sort of pork cooking over the gas fire had already made its rounds to all corners of the small home.

Mi Amá dipped a small towel in salt water and wrapped it around my hand, while she gathered green mint leaves and other plants from her garden. She quickly placed a pot for boiling water on the stove, adding fresh garden greens, cinnamon, mint and *ruda* (a popular remedy plant of México). She also rubbed large pieces of granulated salt onto my hand. I could feel the coarse salt on the surface of my tender, swollen skin. For several weeks, my mother repeated different home-style remedies, occasionally changing the ingredients.

There was no doubt that our family was private about personal matters. We took care of our own problems and made sure not to encroach on other people's busy lives to solve our own matters. This was the manner in which my father set some standards, and we all followed them.

I knew that my hand was not getting any better. As a matter of fact, it was stiffening up on me and settling into a purplish shade. We were poor, and the thought of a doctor was not our first consideration. Besides, the injury seemed not to be a true medical emergency. I could walk, talk, and eat and most importantly, laugh. "No blood, no major medical emergency," was the expectation around our home. In fact, when it came to family health concerns, my mother preferred to take care of us in her own ways. These were the customs that we brought from México. Besides, she was the strong woman who guided us through difficult times.

In her own ways, she reminded us that all of us had been born at home, and, had been cut with the same old scissors. She found some unspoken solace in knowing that the same woman had used the same scissors to cut each of our umbilical cords. *Mi Amá* considered us close to each other because, she always added, "our innards from birth were buried in the same hole"; this was a solid point that showed our family unity.

An Accident

During my first ten years, I rarely visited doctors or received any standard medical attention, other than what the public schools had to offer and what the immigration officials had demanded for our paperwork. Our devoted and patient mother was our nurse. Given the circumstances, she tended to my hand for three weeks after the infamous motorcycle accident. My poor brother Luis was mortified for having caused so many traumas from a simple bike ride.

As part of my Saturday chores, I was responsible for taking pork burritos with beans to my father to share with his *patrones* (bosses) at work. It was a few weeks after our spill during a Saturday visit to the feedlot mill that one of the ranch owners noticed my swollen hand. For what seemed to be a few seconds, he cradled my hand in his own white hands. A silken glaze of tenderness filled the face of this rough, tobacco-chewing man, as he looked intently at the black and purple marks. He then walked me over to where my father was mixing cattle feed. The noisy mill and sweet mixture smell grew louder and stronger, as we neared the huge iron, horse-like motors. The turbines were loud, and louder at close range to the motors.

My father's boss, Jack, pointed toward my busy father and signaled for him to walk to where we stood. The mechanized noise was so fierce that the conversation between the two men was reduced to hand motions. Both men seemed to be yelling at the height of their voices. Jack signaled my father to turn down the engines of the feedlot. "Silvino, this young lady needs attention from a doctor," he yelled at my father. It was the first time I remember somebody calling me a "young lady." I still considered myself a child, because I was the youngest in my whole family.

My obedient and respectful father just nodded his head, affirming what he had heard. As a matter of fact, I do not think I ever saw, heard or noticed any time in which my father disagreed with his *patrón*. I myself could barely hear and understand Jack's English. We had been in the United States long enough for us to capture basic sentences and comprehend and barely understand what was said. For what we did not understand, we politely filled in the blanks with bland, guessed meanings. Those of us in school had no choice but to learn quickly in totally immersed English environments. We all knew my father understood English pretty darn well, but it would be difficult for him to grasp the entire conversation with the motors going full-blast.

My father took out his well-folded, white handkerchief and rubbed his forehead. I knew it was a sign of concern and not a way to wipe the sweat from his forehead. We knew that whenever my father had a situation that caused discomfort, he rubbed his forehead with his long- sleeved shirt. Or if someone was in front of him, he courteously used one of the several squared cotton handkerchiefs my mother so lovingly ironed for him each week.

My father had come to the same painful conclusion as Jack but was not ready to give up on my mother's home-spun "remedies."

My father trusted my mother with all his heart and conviction. He knew my mother had certain powers of healing that every mother probably has with her children. Like a possessive hen, my mother used all her energies to take care of her nine children in such a wonderful manner. Wherever we hurt, my mother would apply warm saliva on the affected area with her soft fingers, repeating, "*Sana, sana, colita de rana. Si no sanas hoy, sanaras mañana*" (Heal, heal, little tail of frog. If you don't heal today, you shall heal tomorrow). It never failed; the pain went away after her touch. With everything she did, my mother also added much faith to the things that concerned all of us.

After several weeks, my hand was developing faint streaks of black and light indigo marks, resisting all of *mi Ama's* efforts to reduce the swelling. She had done everything to help reduce the insatiable swelling.

The following Monday, my father fed the cattle earlier and drove us to Dr. Foster's office in Brawley. *Mi Amá* did not drive and never learned the art of maneuvering through the county traffic. Besides, my mother really did not have the heart to drive. She was happy to have my father taxi her whenever and wherever they went. Also, she realized that knowing how to drive did not add much value to the close-knit family. Moreover, for many years we only had one car.

Dr. Foster was known for his work with the indigent families of the area. His white doctor's robe matched his silvery hair. He was a robust man, willing to see the poorest and most humble patients in the area. Many of his patients did not have money to pay up front; yet Dr. Foster provided the services needed. I guess it was said at the time, that Dr. Foster was the doctor for the Mexicans.

No one knew what to expect from this visit, as we quietly sat and patiently waited for the doctor. I was really nervous, not because of my hand, but because of his constant prescription of castor oil for our ailments. I knew what that meant, and was extremely worried that Dr. Foster would again advise that we take the oil for the cure. My mother's nervousness was apparent. Her tiny, dark-brown eyes held her fears together. Her baby daughter was not healing, and she feared the worst. She knew that something was wrong with my hand, because all the remedies she tried did not work. What made it so difficult was the burden of not knowing English and being in a new country, with a new set of factors relating to medical care not known to us. The heavy emotions of guilt she had maternally laid on me were now reversed, and it was she who was not comfortable with the possible outcome of the motorcycle accident.

Dr. Foster's office was filled with people with expressions similar to that of my mother. A heavy load seemed to be placed on my mother's shoulders, as we waited for the doctor.

The doctor took X-rays of my hand from two different angles. I do not really remember if we waited there for the results or returned at a later date. When Dr. Foster met us again in the examination room, the lights were off to highlight a set of X-rays posted on a lighted board. I suspect that my parent's hearts fell to their feet when they realized the results of the charcoal pictures. It was obvious that I had suffered numerous fractures. The bone shafts of my hand were shattered in different places, forming visible bone deformities. My bones looked like the undernourished twisted roots of a *chayote* (a potato-like vegetable that grows on vines) plant growing every which way. Dr. Foster used the point of his shiny pen to point out the spaghetti-looking mix of bones on the X-ray.

The doctor was calm, and so were my parents' composed postures. They put on strong faces for me, but I could see that they were feeling anguished, and their hearts were heavy from the view of the black and charcoal pictures. I probably should not have been there at this time, but it was customary for us children to do so. We were always included and invited to participate in many adult, English-spoken conversations in order to help facilitate the language barriers. "*Ha qué caray!*" (Oh dear me) were my father's first words. "*Ni modo, que hacemos?*" (Oh well, what can we do?). He spoke softly, shaking his head from one side to the other. My mother's eyes tenderly followed mine, as I interpreted for my parents the outcome of the X-rays. Dr. Foster spoke some Spanish, but his English was much clearer.

The doctor said that the young bone shafts in my hand had to be re-broken and joined again, so that they could grow properly. The doctor took my hand, placed it on the palm of his left hand while he pointed and explained to my parents the results of his analysis. The painful news for my parents was not over; such an operation could not be preformed in the Imperial Valley. My parents were advised that I had to be taken to the Children's Hospital in San Diego, and the sooner the better, the doctor urged. As always and without many questions, my parents agreed to do whatever was necessary. With their consent, the doctor made the appropriate calls for me to be admitted on the following Monday. My parents seemed to take all this in a matter-of-fact way, but, as a child, I did not have the capacity to understand the complex emotional effect of such profound news for a family with limited resources. In addition, they did not understand English well, and so they kept many of their concerns to themselves in order not to upset anyone else in the family.

I did not really know what to expect, since I had never visited a hospital before or been admitted into one. One of my father's main concerns was the long trip to San Diego, which is separated from the Imperial Valley by a ridge of desert lands and mountains. In those days, the trip was a difficult one because of the steep hills. The old-fashioned radiator systems in the cars could barely handle a few hills, let alone a backbone of rocky canyons and sharp ridges. Many cars were left stranded on the hot asphalt, due to radiator problems. In the Imperial Valley in those days, only the rich went to San Diego to get away from the heat of the valley.

Fortunately, my father's red Valiant was up to the task and carried us easily through the hills to San Diego. The trip was long and no doubt sad for my parents. My hand did not hurt as everyone assumed; the broken bones had formed connections as best they could and were adjusting to the troublesome new growth patterns. But my disfigured left hand stood out in comparison to the right one.

The nurses were waiting for us at the hospital. My mother and father must have been anxious. I do not remember going through registration, but I do remember being overwhelmed by the hugeness of the hospital. I had never known before that there were hospitals just for kids like me. Many bright colors decorated the floor and walls, and this place was "kid-friendly."

My parents stayed with me until I was fully admitted. My father had to return to feed the cattle the following morning. I really do not remember a day in which my father took time away from feeding the cattle. On occasion, my father took Saturday afternoons to drive us to Bakersfield to visit Uncle Genaro. Our uncle lived in the town of Lamont. During the brief time away from work, my father asked his co-workers or my older brothers to feed the cattle.

The San Diego round-trip in those days was a full-day event. The surgery was to take place the following morning. At the time of the surgery, I was given some type of injection and inhaled gas through a mask, but the rest is fuzzy. This was the first time I had someone other than my mother, father or brothers put me to sleep. When I woke up the next day, I was alone. My hand was bandaged in a ball of cheesecloth material, and my whole arm was set on pillows, elevating it high above my other.

For the first time in my life, I was actually alone. Economic necessity forced my parents to return to Imperial Valley. How sad it must have been to drive home without their little girl, leaving her in a hospital so far away from home. But what could they do? No doubt, many tears were shed on my mother's pillow during the week I remained in the hospital. It must have taken a tremendous amount of courage on my parents' part to drive me there and drive back without me. I knew in my heart that they always meant well for me; this was no exception. I have always wondered what was said about me by my family during my unexpected and necessary absence.

I, on the other hand, had lots of fun at the hospital. The colorful room was, to my surprise, a wonderful place to be. The nurses all wore white and pink. I could not do much with my left hand, bundled up in gauze and tape, but the food they brought to my room was much better than what we were served in the school cafeteria. The smells of a hospital were so different and foreign to me at the time. The smell of cooking lard and pork was absent. The corn smell of fresh tortillas was also missing from the hospital's sterile environment.

During the day, one of the nurses escorted me to the children's craft room, a treasure-trove of puppets, crafts, movies, coloring books, and toys, toys, and more toys. I remember the difficulty of gluing my mother a pair of silly earrings with one hand. I imagined that she would wear the jewelry for the rest of her life. The tiny, fake stones and diamonds were abundant in the craft room. I also made my first sock puppet, with plastic eyes that moved and a red felt mouth that could say whatever came from my lips. It was the start and inspiration of my life-long love for puppets and ventriloquism.

After almost a week in the hospital, my father and mother returned to San Diego to pick me up. By then, I was ready to go home, anxious to see my mother's excitement about giving her a pair of earrings made of tiny rocks. My parents were overjoyed at seeing me. My mother's eyes welled with tears after she hugged me with a cautious shift of her body to protect my left hand. The sling hanging from my shoulder brought the first signs of concern. On the way back, the mountains seemed mild to all of us, even after my father's car broke down in the middle of the downhill slope. The broken-down car was not a priority, because I was reunited with my family.

I could not be happier. I was waited on hand and foot during my recovery back home in the Imperial Valley. During these days it seemed to me that any teasing of the little sister was off-limits. I was catered to like a "little princess."

A few weeks later, we drove once more across the mountains so that the doctors could remove the long, silver pins that had held the growing bones in my hand. The bones had to fuse together after they had been broken again and placed by the doctors in the proper alignment. The scars on my hand are eternal memories of that eventful day on the dusty side roads next to the canals in Imperial Valley. It is true that many good things can come of painful experiences. I believe that we survive these past experiences with flying colors and grow into what we are today.

It is remarkable how poverty and courage blended in such warm experiences to give us today a treasured memory of an adventure in the past. In spite of all the challenges facing our family at this time, my parents made sure that we were raised to trust and have confidence in the kindness of the people, no matter what social levels they were at.

Several years later, it was my brother Luis who was hurt in Vietnam. It was at that time that I felt so sorry for him being so far away and in the hospital. I saw how much my parents suffered, lamenting his absence and the unseen pain from such a far distance. There is no doubt that children, no matter what age, bring much joy to parents when things are well and a great deal of pain when things are not right.

Tomatoes and Peaches

Our Migrant Experience

1967

We would never have guessed that we were going to
spend the summer of 1967 picking tomatoes and
peaches. We were used to working under the tiring
desert sun in southern California, hoeing the weeds between the
young, flowerless cotton plants. But this summer was special. We
took a memorable trip to Yuba County in the northern part of the
state to work as immigrant fruit pickers.

We were a family of modest means, with my father's income not
enough to pay our family debts. Some of our relatives had done
financially well, picking fruit in the agricultural fields of California,
so my mother convinced my father to permit us to go out and work
as migrants. My father had always pledged that he would not take
his children out of school to pick fruits. He had also lived in many
migrant camps and had no fondness for the hard life there. He did

not want his family to experience the discomfort and unaccommodating conditions of the migrant camps.

My mother was insistent on helping alleviate my father's burden of debt; therefore, she convinced my father to support for working away from the Imperial Valley to contribute more money to the family's economy. It is important to mention that we were already working, cleaning the Rocking Arrow Ranch offices and working summers hoeing cotton. My brothers were also working on weekends as cowhands and in the agricultural fields.

My mother, brother, sister and I packed our bags and left for the Sacramento Valley soon after the last day of school. We had been told to arrive there early to get our names high up on the list of families to be called on to help pick the crops.

As relatively new Americans, many things created challenges for us. We had moved to the United States from a small Mexican village. The corn and bean crops, along with a few cows and chickens, provided our daily foods. Natural mountain beauty surrounded our humble adobe village. In this new, adventurous country, with little money and a large family, my father struggled to make sure we had all we needed. He obtained a credit card from one of the well-known clothing stores and bought school clothes and Christmas presents for all of us. His job at the feedlot did not pay enough to cover those things without him going into debt. His meager salary was far below the average salaries in the sixties.

I am sure he and my mother did not fully understand the cones-
quences of credit cards, especially the high interest rates that are
applied when purchasing good with plastic credit. Understandably
so: we had come from a small village where the closest thing to a
credit card was the United States immigration green card made of
thick plastic that men showed off to others. Inside the light, green
card was the handsome picture of the immigrant. Not many people
in our small village used the Mexican banks in the fifties, since
they were not trusted. Besides, there was no need to work with the
banking institutions unless you had money to save. We did not.

One of the reasons we went to work as migrant laborers in the
summer of 1967 was to help pay off that credit card. My mother
had never worked outside the home before but was determined
to help. Most other Mexican women worked alongside their
husbands and children in the fields, and so my mother wanted to
prove she was capable of picking fruits, too.

When we arrived in Sacramento, the state capital, my brother
Hector set out to find an apartment for us to rent. So many stories
circulated about the conditions of the migrant camps that my
father had instructed my mother to live elsewhere. His experience
had been enough.

A small apartment was found, and we unpacked our simple
belongings to begin work on the farms of Yuba County. We
were called first to the tomato fields, where we were taught
which tomatoes to pick for the packing sheds. The ripe fruits

were everywhere on the dark green, powdery vines that camouflaged them. After working all day, the pungent smell of tomatoes permeated our clothes. Our hands, knees, elbows, and behinds were always stained with red juice.

Overripe tomatoes are extremely volatile when they hit a hard target, and so tomato fights were common among the younger workers in the fields. Like red water balloons, the rotting fruits exploded on contact, causing much laughter and providing a welcome diversion from the routine of hard labor. Remnants of the little bombs dried on our clothes, leaving a network of blood-red vessels that did not come out, even after laundering.

My brother, mother, and older sister worked the hardest. Although fourteen, I was still the baby of the family and could get away with less effort. I enjoyed talking with the other laborers and finding out why they needed to work. I was curious as to why so many young adults worked so hard in such conditions and was surprised to learn that it was a way of life for many of them.

The bathroom facilities were unsophisticated — a one-person wooden structure on tiny rubber wheels was driven on the edge of the field for our use. The portable outhouse contained the toilet waste along the fields while we worked. Inside the tiny, closet-sized structure, I could see the excrement and toilet paper floating underneath the wooden commode. Mixed in the junk were pieces of torn newspaper print, the ink washed away by the ocean of urine. The brutal smell of urine and waste penetrated the wooden planks on the floor, forcing everyone to make every visit a quick one. It was embarrassing to walk from the edge of the field to the platform and climb the two or three steps into the telephone booth-sized outhouse. I felt like everyone was watching.

Just a few yards away, the foremen set up yellow plastic water barrels. Flat paper cones waited for fruit pickers to force them open like tiny dunce caps, turning them into drinking cups. When the paper cups were not available, the more common practice was to tie a tin cup to the water containers. The ice-cold water was an excuse to take a break from the nasty mix of dirt and stinking tomato paste. As we worked our way from one side of the field to the other, the labor foreman wheeled the bathrooms to a close range to the workers in order to keep up with the demands. He also relocated the water coolers to keep up with our direction and pace.

When the tomato season began to slow down, we moved to the peach orchards. Peach-picking was not an easy task. Four of us worked together for the same dollar. My brother climbed a skinny wooden ladder to pick from the tallest branches, wearing a tent-like sack held by straps around his shoulders. When the sack was filled to the rim, my brother carefully stepped down to empty it into large wooden boxes.

My sister also carried a large sack and worked close to my brother. My sister Blanca was no weakling, and she was going to reach her goals through her ability to compete with any one in the fields.

My mother attributed her energetic development to the raw eggs that she easily quaffed. She was competitive and fiercely strong. Her classmates even called her the "Jolly Green Giant." My mother and I picked the peaches growing on the lowest branches. I was also responsible for retrieving the fruit that fell to the ground. We would briefly celebrate at the filling of the huge wooden boxes. A tractor came by periodically to drop off empty boxes for more peaches.

Peaches were not as dirty or messy as tomatoes, and the smell was more tolerable. The worst part was the layer of pesticide dust covering every green leaf. In those days, no one asked about the potential dangers of such chemicals, and nobody wore masks or gloves. Most of us carried large, colorful handkerchiefs to cover our noses and mouths on windy days, making us look like bandits robbing the trees of their valuables. When we stopped work at the end of the day, we simply shook the grey dust from our clothes and hair, and more dust came off during the daily showers.

Yuba County was not as hot as the Imperial Valley, where we were accustomed to a summer dawn temperature of 70°F that climbed to 120°F at mid-afternoon. In Yuba County, we left our apartment hours before dawn to be ready when the first light made the peaches visible. Those early hours were cold for us. Fifty-degree weather felt like freezing to our desert-rat skin.

While we lived in Sacramento that summer, we did get a taste of soft ice cream after the hot work days, and we visited the

California State Fair. But when most children were going to the theater to see *The Sound of Music*, we were stuck in the tomato and peach fields. It was not a painful experience, but I realized that I would rather work in 120-degree heat in the cotton fields than in the tomato fields and peach orchards.

The most difficult aspect of our migrant experience was coming home to an apartment surrounded by cemented walls. The absence of green fields or grass and salt cedar trees made me homesick. The smell of fresh-cut alfalfa was no longer present. In the Imperial Valley, I could go home after hoeing the cotton fields and walk out into the open air to collect my thoughts. I did not like a crowded world with nothing but four walls, a loud alarm clock and a small black and white television.

Many of my classmates in the Imperial Valley left during the summers to pick grapes from the vines in the cooler weather of the Delano area. They always returned with stories of their migrant experiences that seemed made-up to me. Talk of shacks and camps and canned food served cold for lunch in the middle of the fields was unbelievable. It was not until we had our own migrant experience that my classmates' stories matched the colorful pictures in my own mind. I clearly remember my good friend, Frank Leones, left every summer with his family to pick table grapes. Frank would write to me relating his grape picking days near Bakersfield, California.

We did not do as well as other families that summer, since we spent most of the money we earned on renting an apartment instead of living in the migrant camps. Back at home, I heard my father and mother talking about the summer and coming to realize that there had not been much real monetary benefit from our experience. A few hundred dollars more had helped, but did not provide any lasting solution to our family's financial burden of keeping up with six growing and changing young adults. We never again left the Valley to work as migrants again. We continued to work in the cotton fields and at the Rocking Arrow Ranch to help our parents. My older brothers worked most weekends to provide the additional needed support to my parents and the entire family.

English Only, Please!

1961

Going to America was a hope and a dream for the grown men and women of our village. For the children, the dream was gradually understood from the collection of conversations heard emanating over and over from the adults in our small village. Once in the United States of America, for children, the first formal encounter with the American dream was at the English-only-speaking schools.

Hundreds and thousands of immigrant children enrolled in American schools at about the same time that our family immigrated to California. In our family, four of us enrolled in elementary and middle school. Alfonso, the fifth youngest, was too old to be enrolled in public school; he began working at the feedlot with my father. Being the youngest, I was enrolled in the first-grade at Niland Elementary School in the northern edge of Imperial Valley. I know for a fact that all of us were placed in grades below our age level because of our *"no sabe hablar Inglés"* (does not know how to speak English) language limitations.

At the age of seven, like any average child, I belonged in the second-grade. In those days, most recent immigrants were placed in grades below their age levels. Knowledge of the English language was the only assessment for students' academic placement in the schools. The schools basically did what they thought was the best thing for those of limited knowledge about language learning. In many cases, they did nothing.

The consequences of the inconsistent age and grade-level placement of non-English speakers were not immediately felt. It was later in the pupils' schooling that noticeable differences became visible, as the students, including myself, began to develop much more quickly than friends and classmates.

My parents trusted Niland Elementary School with their four youngest children. Since no one in my family understood how placement decisions were made, my parents never questioned our grade placement. It was not their style to question the education experts of this great country. It was also part of our nature and culture to respect the experts in the other various fields including medicine. Besides, it was well understood that we were guests in the United States. My father would say that in order to be more than guests in the United States, we had to learn how to speak the language and then work harder then everyone else in order to get ahead. Even so, the strongest organization known to

us, our family, was the only strength and support of our early
efforts to learn some limited, English- speaking skills.

Not much bothered us, and we did not feel any less than anyone
around us. The only difference was in the words that came out
of our mouths. Mostly everyone around us spoke English, and
Spanish was not allowed in our classes. Early on in our new
school, we heard that speaking in Spanish was punished. We also
knew that if we were punished at school, our parents found out.
Therefore, we spoke only a few words of Spanish during the school
day. "English only" was constantly being repeated by teachers in
different grade- levels. Although we did not give it much thought,
we were determined to find a middle ground that included both
languages. We were eager to please at school and eager to receive
praise from our parents and older siblings.

In our family, we knew who was boss. Our father was the ultimate
authority, followed by my mother. At school, we knew the teacher
was in charge. For our first day ever in an American school, our
father took time from work to drive us from our country home.
For the remaining eight years, a large yellow bus drove through
the country roads, making many stops along the way. Our stop
was one of the last before the dusty bus made its way to the school.
In the afternoons, our bus stop was last on the route. During some
years, our school bus stop was one of the first.

On rainy days, the clay roads were too muddy for the bus to
navigate. On these days, we had to walk a little more than a

quarter of a mile to the paved road to wait for the bus. On numerous occasions, our bus got stuck in the mud, and our adven-tures
were retold over and over at school and at home. The best part
was arriving late to school, having to spend more time outside the
classroom shaking the mud from our shoes. Everyone in the
classroom, including the teachers, wanted to hear about our school
bus adventures on rainy and muddy days.

One lucky rainy day, one of our father's bosses was driving by in
his white pickup, as we started to walk toward the paved road. He
signaled for us to hurry onto his truck. I fondly remember him
getting out of his pickup to assist me with my shoes. I did not want
to keep my shoes or socks on, because they would get muddy, so I
took them off and walked barefooted to the paved road. There I
took a stick and scraped the mud off my feet and ankles. The big
chunks of mud fell off as I suavely swept the stick from my leg
down to the ankle and off at the heel; it was as if I was spreading
mud-colored cream cheese frosting on my legs. Thin streaks of
mud remained on me until the bus stopped in front of our school.
At school, I used wet paper towels to rub the brown mud lines left
from the stick scraping off my legs. I was glad the contemporary
mud art was washable.

Unlike our school experience in México, we did not go home for
lunch or for our mid-day break. In México, school was held from
early morning to early afternoon. In the United States, for
students living in rural areas, the school day started at dawn and
ended after five in the afternoon. In México, our mother always

had some type of clay pots on the open hearth with beans and rice and boiled milk. Life and school were going to be very different in our new environment.

As we slowly settled in our new country home, my mother continued to masterfully cook the tasty foods that sparked our appetite. It took only a few feet of walking from the front or back door until the garlic and onion smell greeted us on our return from school. When all of us got off the bus, I distinctly recall my brother Hector and sister Blanca racing for one of the house doors. It was a constant competition to see who got to the kitchen first.

Niland Elementary School mirrored a true melting pot. Students from a variety of cultures and backgrounds became our classmates and friends. In the mid-1900s, many Filipinos began migrating to Niland, California, to labor for Southern Pacific and work in the agricultural fields of tomatoes, sugar beets, and cotton. There were also Anglo students with Midwest roots in Niland. Recent Chinese and Korean immigrants also made Niland their new home. My classmates were descendents of many cultures and countries. While most of my classmates spoke better English than I, the school did an excellent job at integrating us into the American culture. Learning in such a diverse environment certainly had some advantages that positively affected me many years later.

In the early 1960s, no federal assistance was offered in school systems to help children learn English. English as a Second Language (ESL) programs or shelter-type classes did not exist.

At my elementary school, there were no teachers who would hold my hand forever, or for that matter, there were no teachers specially dedicated to those of us who belonged to the "*no habla Inglés*" club. It was not until Title VII was enacted in 1964 that school districts had access to federal funds to help non-English-speaking immigrant students. Nevertheless, it took several years before the help was provided specifically for the "*no habla Inglés*" child.

How in the world did we learn the new language of the North Americans, *Americanos, Gabachos* and *Gringos* (we used these terms often before we left México)? In our small village, these words were not as insulting as they are currently perceived to be by some in many parts of the country. On the contrary, in our village, these words were powerful ones to describe the important, rich, and lucky people who lived in America, the land of plenty. We, on the other hand, were not as fortunate as the "Americanos." Our humble "*milpa*" (cornfield) was not able to produce enough "*maiz,* (corn), *calabazas* (squash) or *frijoles* (beans)" for the hungry family. Had it not been for my father's early dollars flowing back to México, we would have been in worse conditions. Our motherland and country of origin could not provide our parents the jobs needed to lift the family out of poverty, and so, like many before, we came to America.

I found myself in what is now called a total-immersion learning environment. I never referred to my education as a "total-immersion" process until after I began teaching students English as a classroom teacher. As a child, I welcomed the educational methods that I experienced as the norm. Never do I remember thinking that I should be instructed in any language-learning method other than the one that would lead me to English. My parents never really questioned the methods of the then-experts in education. Knowing my parents, I do not think they would question the experts today, either. Today, we know that the "one size method" for learning English does not meet every child's language learning needs. In the self-contained classrooms (one teacher with the same students for the entire day), no Spanish was spoken. I must admit, there were a few members of the staff who prohibited us from speaking Spanish, but it was rare that we spoke Spanish, and then only when a new "*no habla Inglés*" student arrived at our school for the first time. Everything at school was in English: the signs, the words, the songs and the books.

After many years, total-immersion was also referred to as the "sink-or-swim" method of learning English. I learned to swim fast enough to finish the race, but at first I was slow and clumsy at communicating what I was thinking. My greatest advantage was my age. I was young and highly self-motivated to fit into the competitive world of the *Americanos*.

My early success pleased my parents much, and that was enough for me to adjust as quickly as possible. The first onion-paper certificate I received was at the end of my first-grade and first year in school. The simple certificate was recognition for my early artistic talent in the first-grade. I must have been good with the sturdy yellow pencil and colored chalk. It was no surprise to my mother, since she had spent many hours showing me how to draw pansies. She lovingly insisted on my learning to draw.

The work of pronouncing sounds and gluing them together to form words was rather difficult for me. My young tongue was getting used to rolling the "r's" and sounding the "n" and "ll" in Spanish. Now I also had to learn to differentiate between "sh" as in "show" and "ch" as in "China." With the fact that the Spanish language has no "sh," it was rather difficult to pronounce. One of the most frequent mistakes I remember making, even in high school, was that of calling out to the teacher or student passing out paper that I needed a "cheet" of paper. I was most embarrassed when I had to speak to pronounce the name of my classmate, "Chet." The mispronunciations of words that I spoke were not at all intentional, but I was in the process of formulating sounds and words and making sure that they were in some type of acceptable order and sound.

I, like most other non-English-speaking students, trusted my ears to hear the sounds I was to regurgitate with meaning and comprehension. Obviously, my ears did their best, but my mouth and tongue twisted sounds a little differently from those spoken by English speakers. I remember going home and my mother suggesting that the cleansing of my ears helped with understanding the teachers' and classmates' spoken sounds. I really never thought of washing my mouth as another effort to speak more like the rest of the classmates; perhaps I should have tried it.

I knew I was not pronouncing words totally correctly. I could see and feel that I was not pronouncing words correctly as they spilled out, but I eagerly tried to be included in America's mainstream. Besides, that is what my father wanted, too. As the baby of the family, I was going to do everything possible to please my father and make my mother proud.

Our parents did not understand the educational system in America, and the only way to inform our parents of our success was to bring home evidence they could clearly see and feel with their own eyes and hands. They did not have a clue about the testing systems and assessments in achievement of public schooling. They did not have a way to measure our progress and achievement other than to see it for themselves. The ability to speak English was one way to demonstrate success, especially to our father, who could understand much more English than we knew at that time. We also learned that bringing home paper certificates, trophies, awarded ribbons and embroidered patches promoted a message of accomplishment with our parents.

The skill that I was able to master quickly was that of observing and interpreting the messages I gathered from the body language, non-verbal motions of the face and, in particular, from the motion of the hands and eyes. I quickly learned to identify the non-verbal signs of approval and discomfort in other people. Despite not understanding the meaning of the words spoken in English, I knew whether people speaking were on a positive or on a negative track. I quickly learned to be silent when the classroom air was filled with tense moments and verbal exchanges between adults and students.

For the first three to five years, I spent many hours intently observing people and focusing on their visual, non-verbal communication. Their smiles, their eyes and their gestures were important to understand, since I could not comprehend the meaning of words. I was glad that a shaking of the head up and down or side-ways meant the same thing in Spanish as it did in English. It was a plus to come from a happy childhood, with happy parents and a happy family. The constant search for humor in the things that we did in our new country brought many smiles and laughs as we integrated into the mainstream of our new home. And so life in America began with my learning English by utilizing a variety of internal learning elements of my human body. I believe we all have these elements, and some of us are forced to use them quickly and effectively. One habit that I acquired during my early years in school was to observe the shoes that people wore. Part of this observation dealt with going to the bathroom and listening to the foreign sounds that people made speaking to each other. By knowing who wore what shoes, I was able to tell who was next to me in the different stalls. Knowing who wore what shoes also made me feel comfortable. To this day, I observe shoes as a left-over vestige of learning new sounds in America.

One day, my father asked me a question about my English learning. "When you dream, do you dream in English or Spanish?" he asked as he went about his daily time-off from everything to read the newspaper in English. I do not remember exactly what I answered, but it must have been funny to him because he looked at me and smiled before returning to the lines of black ink on the paper. In fact, today, I think the phrase in Spanish and speak it in English, or think in Spanish and write in English. As a child, I did not give much thought to the learning process.

At an early age, I used to invent English words to make up for words I did not know. We were also put on the spot by family members who did not speak or understand English. When we visited México, these family members wanted a sample of words in English. They wanted to hear the foreign words they had never heard before. Without electricity, radios, televisions and contact with Americans, people in our Mexican village of La Yerbabuena were filled with curiosity about the English language and wanted to hear what it sounded like; they did this by asking us how to say certain words. Now, to my chagrin, I remember making up sounds to please relatives who had never heard English before.

On one visit to México, I remember being asked to sing something in English. I began to sing, "Glory, glory hallelujah, glory, glory hallelujah," not thinking much about what people might say. Amazingly, my mother got word that we were being converted to another religion because I was singing a church song with some "hallelujah- type" verse. The women in Mexican shawls were chitchatting about the possibility that we were being driven away from the Catholic religion in the United States because of the song

I had recently learned and shared with my Mexican relatives. My mother instructed me to be careful about what I said, because people did not understand English in our village.

When I played with the dolls and the birds, I used to speak to them in my own made-up "Spanglish" (half Spanish, half English) words, pretending I was really saying something important. I remember my brothers asking "You *sabe mucho* English?" I would answer, "Yes, *me sabe mucho* English." I believe we all struggled early on with our language limitations.

When we sang in school, I added sounds to pretend I was singing along with everyone else. I was also glad early on to hear familiar words in songs. The word "Montezuma" sounded so much like the frequently used Spanish word "*Moctezuma.*" An occasional, familiar word brought a welcome sense of security.

Some say that learning effective English in the "sink or swim" manner is horrible and unfair. Some say that the system was insensitive to our needs, but I do not think it was intentional. I do not think the Niland Elementary School staff and teachers at Imperial Valley wanted to exclude us from anything, or forced us into anything, either. It was the appropriate thing to do for that particular time and place in education. Was the teaching of English present in our elementary schools? Probably not. I can say that perhaps for some students, this method of total immersion is not an effective manner of teaching or learning without some interventions, but for me and my brothers, it worked. In our home, we were expected to learn, no matter what the conditions were at school or in the classroom. Expectations proved to be a powerful motivational tool. Excuses were not acceptable to our parents when it came any topic of learning and education.

Niland Elementary School was multi-ethnic, and that was a major plus for us. In addition, there were other students like us who did not speak English. I do not remember ever being pulled out of class to study English with a small group of non-English speakers with support from an adult bilingual aide. In fact, our learning of English was so smooth that it was not until I got to high school that I noticed other students struggling with the learning of the new language. Perhaps our greatest advantage in the process of learning English was enrolling in school at such an early age.

Early on, my limitations in the correct pronunciations and spelling, along with my Spanish accent, gave me away as a foreigner. It was in high school that I felt a bit unequal to others. I never let anyone know I had these feelings, but I did know that I was different in many aspects. However, these feelings of being different did not keep me from being involved in school activities and programs. Perhaps my relationship with my family was so strong that my relations at school were secondary, although I enjoyed my friends much, and we shared many great experiences together. In terms of importance, school classmates were not at the top of the list.

English is so difficult, because the sounds change, and the rules of pronunciation are not consistent, unlike most of the sounds in Spanish. I did not know how to read Spanish until I was in the fourth-grade. The schools did not teach Spanish, but my father always managed to introduce us to Spanish-written newspapers. My mother sat with me at the kitchen table and sounded out the letters in Spanish. The Spanish- alphabet always uses the same sounds for the different letters and vowels. Many years later, my father encouraged me to write articles for a regional newspaper in Michoacán, México. Thanks to my father's inspiration and support, I became a contributor of articles written in Spanish of our American experiences. For several years afterwards, I heard from Mexican newspaper fans who were hungry to read more about my childhood experiences and cultural differences between Mexicans and Americans.

I do remember that my ability to compete in early grades was more difficult than later in life. I remember spending much of my time watching others and hearing English spoken so fast that it seemed to me the speakers quickly swallowed the words to the gut of their stomach. Those that did not understand Spanish asked us to speak slower so that they could understand some of the meanings. I intently watched many mouths move rapidly in the language that I could not totally comprehend.

As I have said, in the first-grade, I won certificates for my abilities in art. Thanks to my mother, I had learned to draw free-hand. When my mother sat at the kitchen table to write letters to relatives in México, she also drew flowers on her writing tablet. I remember in particular the pansies and sunflowers, varieties that were popular in México. By imitating her, I learned to draw. I won awards for my art, but not for my English.

By the fourth-grade, I had become involved in various sports programs at school. I enjoyed running and participating in competitive events. I won awards in sports, but not in English. By the time I graduated from eighth-grade, I had received numerous awards in a variety of school events and subjects— but never in English subjects.

The first English-written book I read was about Jim Thorpe, the great Olympian. Jim Thorpe's story was so motivating that I spent an entire year reporting and sharing his ordeal with other classmates. Reading books and stories relating to people and sports really enthused me. Thanks for literacy, I had set my goals of becoming a teacher and before becoming too old, I wanted to travel throughout world.

Learning English often was made difficult by my biased listening skills, or the unfamiliar intonations of the speakers. I was often laughed at for innocent mispronunciations. But learning English is a life-long process. How silly of me to think that after I graduated from high school or college, my English would be perfect. Learning English involves so much practice and perseverance, so much reinforcement and acceptance, as well as recognition and patience. Music played an important role in my learning. I did not know much English, but my mistakes and accent could be hidden in the loud, joyous chorus of our weekly choral classes.

I happily recalled many songs: "I've been working on the railroad all the live-long day,"; "Row, row, row your boat gently down the stream,"; "I am a Yankee Doodle Dandy, Yankee Doodle do or die,"; "She'll be coming' round the mountain when she comes. She'll be coming' round the mountain when she comes,"; "From the halls of Montezuma to the shores of Tripoli,"; "Glory, glory hallelujah, glory, glory hallelujah,"; "O beautiful for spacious skies, for amber waves of grain, for purple mountain majesties,"; "This land is your land, this land is my land,"; and the famous "Old MacDonald had a farm, e-i-e-i-o. And on that farm, he had a cow, e-i-e-i-o." These songs united the classroom in one voice without focusing on the differences of cultures, statuses, or languages. English music was heard at home too. The Wilkinson family had given my father boxes of used clothing and 78 RPM records with Johnny Cash and Tony Bennett's music. We heard many of the outdated late fifties songs in records no longer wanted by the daughters of my father's bosses. We were soon repeating the words in the records, although we did not understand the words. The music was "catchy."

I firmly believe that what helped me the most was the acknowledgment and support from others that I was making a sincere effort to speak English. In the fourth-grade, for example, I entered one of my first speech contests. I know now that I butchered the language with poorly organized and mispronounced phrases. It must have been a comedy act for some of the people in the audience. However, I do not remember people laughing at me. I did not win this particular speech contest, but in the future did place in other contests. Competing was not just about winning awards; it was about being part of those that tried.

I was in high school when I realized that I did not know as much English as other students. For that matter, I knew provincial, limited and poorly pronounced English. My language skills were not good enough for placement in the advanced math and science courses. I had concentrated too much on the words out of context and had not spent enough time comprehending the content of the subject matter.

I often watched the academic material roll by like scenery passing on the outside of a fast-moving train. I did not have the appropriate understanding of the entire meaning of the full English sentences and paragraphs. I realized that I had missed out on the early content discussions of Shakespeare, Einstein, Washington and Lincoln.

For a few years, I felt I was not prepared to understand the academic content of the early grade-level discussions. But my overriding hunger to succeed ultimately translated into learning English. Success in the English language meant that my parents would be proud of me. Learning English also meant that I could help them on the many occasions when they needed someone to translate for them. We were expected to help by translating the spoken English of doctors, bankers, store clerks and teachers into Spanish. I needed to learn English in order to succeed in America. I did not expect to have Americans learn Spanish to accommodate my limitations.

It was not easy to navigate through the myriad rules of the English language and at the same time understand the full content of the messages that went through the ears and mouths of children. I had to translate any and all communication into Spanish in order to understand most of the meanings. We were the guests in the United States, and English was a must.

My desire to learn English was not just an academic goal. Learning English also meant making new friends and sharing enjoyable classroom activities. As a child from a large family, I sense that being part of a group was important. Deep inside me, the need to be included was more important than to feel unique. I also wanted to be successful, and that determination provided an important level of energy, accelerating the speedy integration of two languages. There is no doubt that language-learning is truly a life-long and life-changing process.

Special Teachers in My Life

Elementary School

1961–1968

In elementary school, I had three male teachers who, though different from each other, had expertise in education and were able to teach me some real lessons.

Mr. Palmer was my fourth-grade teacher. He must have been about thirty-five years old, but his flat-top haircut and beer belly made him look older. He was an impatient reading teacher who much preferred math. He especially enjoyed working on science projects with his students.

I was already twelve years old and curious about everything. I wanted to learn about animals and anatomy, but that was not to be. In Mr. Palmer's class, we focused on building models to prove that electricity travels. Mr. Palmer focused on nails and wires. I am certain that we studied other scientific things from time to time, but Mr. Palmer could not get away from his shop-teacher approach to instruction.

For one assignment, he provided the entire class with a list of supplies needed for an electrical current project. We were to bring in electrical wire, wood blocks, and large nails. In addition, we were to supply a large battery the size of a can of baking powder.

I was very fortunate to live in the country near a ranch that included a huge tin building filled with electrical supplies. The ongoing construction of corrals at the feedlot meant that many wood blocks were also available for my school project. I took extra wood blocks, nails, and wire for other students who did not have easy access to the required materials.

Although my parents' limited English prevented them from communicating fully with my teachers, my father and mother were always willing to help collect or purchase materials needed for school projects. In addition, Teofilo, my father's best friend at the feedlot, was an expert welder. For this project, he shared with me some of his knowledge of electricity. I felt quite proud of my skills, as I showed my classmates how to connect the wires correctly to form an electrical current.

Another time, all of Mr. Palmer's students were required to create a show-and-tell type of science project. My class presentation involved bringing in materials from the cowboy shop at the feedlot. For this science project, I solicited the help of my big brother, who worked with the horses and cattle at the feedlot. He loaned me some instruments used to force-feed medicine to the cattle. These instruments were long, stainless-steel rods with an open space at one end fitted to hold the special cow pills. I also took syringes to show the students the large needles used to immunize new arrivals to the cattle hotel. Along with the syringes, I showed my classmates the large medicine bottles filled with pale white serum for the animals.

I borrowed several types of pills that my brother used for different medical reasons. Although he was not a veterinarian by trade, he was considered one by experience. The huge, white pills generated the most "oh's and ah's" during the presentation. I stuck a three-inch pill halfway into my mouth just to be silly, wanting to demonstrate that I was not afraid of cow medicine. My demonstration got big laughs from the boys and silly smirks from the girls.

To close my presentation, I brought out a tin pail with a rubber teat stuck to the base of the container. This pail, I explained, was to feed any calves that were accidentally delivered at the feedlot. My contribution to show-and-tell was well received by Mr. Palmer and the other students and provided much discussion and interest for months to come. My classmates thought I really lived in a fantastic location compared to their remote, small town of Niland. I, on the other hand, felt envious towards them for living close to town, able to participate in all the great after-school activities.

Mr. Fluke's fifth-grade class was something else altogether. A thin, bald man, Mr. Fluke reminded me of the rider in the tale of the "Headless Horseman." He looked out of place in the desert, dressing every day in a crisp white shirt, dark suit, and tie. In addition to teaching fifth-grade, he also taught music. Thanks to Mr. Fluke, I began to play the trumpet. While Mr. Fluke was not able to control the class well, he was, however, a good music teacher. His face always became bright and happy during music lessons.

Mr. Fluke had little time for needed and expected discipline. He was passionate about music and focused on it so much that the management of the rest of the class was left to the students, who made up their own rules of comportment. The bullies of the class were in charge of the school year. The disorganization provided cover for the bullies in the class to browbeat the weaker students. Crazy things happened in Mr. Fluke's classroom, and his band practices seemed to go on forever. It was no surprise that he did not return for a second year at Niland.

My eighth-grade teacher was Mr. Duke. A handsome and athletically-built man in his early twenties, Mr. Duke was kind to all the students. Unlike Mr. Fluke, he worked hard to fit in at the school. The girls liked him for his good looks, and the boys admired his active style. He often took the class outside to play ball and even joined us during sports-team competitions. He had come to Niland School from San Fernando Valley, a suburb of Los Angeles. We always wondered why he left the big city to teach in the middle of the desert, but were glad he did. He was energetic and looked a great deal like Robert Redford.

In Mr. Duke's class, we played games inside and outside the classroom. His forté was history, and so we focused on the history of the United States. We also spent countless hours working with maps to learn geography. Not much writing or reading took place in Mr. Duke's class, but he motivated us to learn and did not tolerate our ill manners. He, too, left Niland a year or two later.

In the eighth-grade, I had my first opportunity to take the lead in the school's play. I played the role of Mrs. Bisbee, a mother of many children and few resources. The play revolved around a bleak Christmas season forcing the family to do with little and to limit Christmas to the joy of being together. This Christmas play in the eighth-grade almost mirrored our own first few Christmas seasons in the Imperial Valley. The play was a success with the student audience and families.

By the eighth-grade, I knew that I wanted to become a teacher and a coach. I also knew that someday I wanted to travel the world and learn about other countries and cultures. Someday, I would see the world from outside the Imperial Valley.

Barbara Jarrett

"Apples of Gold"

1969

An unexpected turn of events caused some challenges in my life, as I turned sixteen. A recession in the cattle industry ended my father's twenty-year job at the Rocking Arrow Ranch. I had just graduated from Niland Elementary School and was looking forward to entering Calipatria High School in the autumn. Unfortunately, we had to give up our beloved country home only miles between Niland and Calipatria.

My brother-in-law, Tommy, provided the next breath of financial hope for the family. He and my oldest sister made their home in the suburbs of Los Angeles, and they took us in. Their house was carpeted, and the green-trimmed yard was a welcome change from the dry desert. We had never lived in a home with soft, carpeted floors. The front door had a small, rectangular hole with a brass-plated cover through which the postman could drop the mail.

They did not need a post office box like the one we had in Calipatria. Our post office box was "545," Calipatria, 92233 for many years. We thought my sister was really lucky to have married someone who could afford a house with carpet and a pretty green yard with tropical plants. It made me think that the city was a rather nice place to live.

At age fifty-five, my father thought he was too old to get another job. But my brother-in-law, a supervisor at a major steel plant, was able to get him an entry-level position there. So we moved to the city, and I enrolled in a city school. To my dismay, I ended up in a junior high school again. In the city school system, the junior high included the ninth-grade, and high school started with the tenth. For the first time in my life, I did not feel confident about myself. I was supposed to be in high school, not junior high! At North Park Junior High School, I felt old around my classmates. In fact, I was older than most ninth-graders. My age difference increased my discomfort. My life seemed to have taken a downturn along with the cattle business.

North Park Junior High School was huge. My junior high in the desert had been a small school with a single class of students in each grade- level. Every student was known by name. In the new school in Pico Rivera, we were grouped by the first letter of our last names. At first, I did not know anyone, and no one knew me. This bothered me in the beginning, but I soon forgot about being new.

During the first school officer's election, I ran for student body vice-president. I don't know what I was thinking at the time; I should have known that the Junior High political machine was already in place. In retrospect, I was probably looking to fit in with the new student population and was not afraid to try new things. I remember losing the race against Elaine Phillips. I had no regrets, as this provided me another way to reach out and meet new classmates.

Another unwanted change was happening in my life. My body was maturing and growing out of my desired shape. I was no longer the skinny track competitor and sit-up champ. Living in the city discouraged much physical activity. We did not have to walk far for anything. My body was growing every which way. My dresses still fit at the top but not at the bottom. I realized for the first time that I had extra layers of fat on my hips, and I was disappointed that I never wore the clothes that Twiggy modeled. I did not understand the developmental changes I was experiencing, and this also hurt my self-confidence. I missed the easy acceptance by my peers and teachers that I had enjoyed in the small desert school.

Most of all, I missed country living and the red-winged birds' songs. The outdoors were limited to the backyard at my sister's house, unlike in the country, where the open fields stretched like eagles' wings to carry me far from human voices. The memory of the desert wind blew a void through my life. But I kept those feelings to myself, protected at the edges of my heart.

Like most female students in school at that time, my choices for elective courses were limited to a few. As a ninth-grader, I could choose between homemaking and typing, according to the school counselor. I definitely did not want to learn how to sew or make cookies. I already helped my mother enough in the kitchen, and sewing was common in our home, so I chose typing. Besides, I found my father's jobs more exciting.

My typing class was located on the second floor of one of the several buildings that made up the large school. Because this was in the late 1960s, the classroom was filled with manual typewriters. Mrs. Jarrett, the typing teacher, was a pretty young woman with light-brown hair. Her smile came straight from her heart. She made me feel wanted during that difficult time of change. She was patient with her clumsy students and kept her class organized. Her students, mostly girls, were well-behaved.

Mrs. Jarrett and I became good friends. I had so much respect for her and for the way she taught her typing class. Mrs. Jarrett seemed to like me too. She greeted me with her nice smile and often asked me to pass out the graded typing test papers. Her kindness made my time there more enjoyable and fulfilling in many ways. I often helped her before and after school to place assignments on the typewriters for the next class.

Mrs. Jarrett was the type of teacher that students always remember not just for being a good teacher, but also because she was a good person. In those days, typing students were graded on the number of errors made during a two-minute typing race.

During the warm-up, timed exercises, the sound of the newly introduced electric typewriters was invigorating and exhilarating. The typing class was like being in a race car everyday. Mrs. Jarrett helped us succeed by carrying a small alarm clock as she walked through the room. I wanted to impress her, so I worked hard to make sure I typed quickly and accurately.

One day, I confided in her that I was not feeling happy at school. I told her about the beauty of the desert and the wonderful opportunity for privacy it offered. I shared with her my view of my world as it pertained to the way my body seemed to be stretching out of control and around the wrong places. This was something that I would not confide in my mother since I seemed to be so natural and so loved at home. With soothing words of support, Mrs. Jarrett encouraged me to visit the school counselor. She assured me that if anyone could help, he was the one. I had never met a school counselor before and was not sure what to expect.

It was shortly before Thanksgiving when I finally spoke to Mr. Hogan. I explained to him that I was too old to be at North Park. This was the only credible reason I could think to offer, not wanting to mention the physical changes rapidly taking over my body. In these cases, parents should be the ones to advocate for their children, but my parents could not. They did not speak English, and I knew they believed that asking questions created problems for the school. My parents would not deal with matters that were not emergencies. They assumed that the school knew what it was doing. Besides, school decisions were always final.

The counselor's small office was decorated with walnut furniture with tall files next to the desk. Behind the desk sat a thin man in his late twenties who listened attentively to my story. His starched white shirt and black tie added to my feeling that I was pleading an important business matter.

North Park was not a school near the border. Even though most of the students were Mexican-American, the school had little experience with immigrants. Most of the students had been born and reared in the community. I explained to Mr. Hogan that I was too old to be in junior high school. When we arrived in the United States from México, the children in our family were placed two grades below our age level because we did not speak English. I was seven and should have been placed in the second or third-grade because of my September birthday. Instead, I had been placed with students much younger than I. In ninth-grade, I was already sixteen.

Mr. Hogan promised to look into promoting me to the next grade-level at the beginning of the second semester. Although he told me I had to wait to find out for sure, I was thrilled. Deep down in my heart, I knew that Mrs. Jarrett had spoken to him on my behalf. In January 1969, I was moved into the tenth-grade at El Rancho High School. Students there had attended various junior high schools in the area. North Park was just one of several "feeder schools" to El Rancho. In less than six months, I had gone from a small class-room of eighth-graders in the rural desert to a big-city class of tenth-graders, numbering in the hundreds.

During my high school and college years, Mrs. Jarrett and I kept in touch. She was a great inspiration to me. I had someone else besides my family that I wanted to make happy. Upon graduation from junior college in Niland, I received a gift from her. She sent me a graduation card and a book of poems and quotes, *Apples of Gold*. *Apples of Gold* is my constant reminder of the teacher who was there for me during a difficult time in my life.

In 1999 I began looking for Mrs. Jarrett again. I called North Park Junior High School, as well as the school district offices. No one remembered the soft-spoken typing teacher. She was the type of teacher who often goes unnoticed. Complaints from parents were few, because she did a great job at teaching and improving typing skills.

No one seemed to know where Ms. Jarrett had moved. I finally decided to contact a popular search agency. For nine months, I received different requests for further information on locations and schools dates pertaining to Mrs. Jarrett. Before Thanksgiving in 2000, another letter arrived from the search agency. Tears rolled down my cheeks as I read that Barbara Jarrett had passed away somewhere in Arizona. I still do not believe or do not want to believe that she has died.

At least in spirit, Mrs. Jarrett is still out there. Even though I often told her how much I appreciated her, I do not think she ever knew that my career led me into education. I will continue to seek the woman whose smile brought me much peace. Every student has a favorite teacher and mentor; mine was Ms. Barbara Jarrett. All teachers and other school employees play an important role in our development. I treasure both the good and the not-so-good experiences I had at Niland Elementary School. I am also grateful for having had Mr. Palmer, Mr. Fluke and Mr. Duke as teachers, who shared their knowledge from different perspectives. In middle school and in high school, I also had teachers of great influence. The men and women of El Rancho High School who were most influential included: Mr. Reno (chemistry teacher), Mr. Matt Miletich (activities director), Mr. Sandoval (counselor), Anita Reyna (activities clerk) and Mr. Duane Reidenbach (track and cross-country coach). Again, however, my warm thanks to the most remembered teacher of my compulsory education experience, Mrs. Jarrett.

Competition

El Rancho High School Track

1970

Can you imagine not being allowed to compete for a varsity letter in your favorite sport? Before Title IX legislation was enacted in 1972, most high school girls who played sports did so only at their own schools. Girls' sport contests or competition between schools were non-existent. Boys, on the other hand, competed in a variety of freshman, junior varsity, and varsity sports during the fall and spring seasons. Not being able to compete in girls' sports was a great disappointment to me.

By the time I was in the eighth-grade, during recess I was the only girl playing hardball with the boys. I began to love playing sports and the competition in early elementary school. We could not wait to swallow the cold and tasteless cafeteria food and rush out to the far end of the schoolyard. A pitcher, a batter, a catcher, and everyone else took the field. We took turns hitting the small hardball with all our might. Whoever caught the ball earned the next chance at hitting it. Most of my female classmates thought I was a tomboy, and perhaps I was, but their teasing did not bother me, because I loved sports. I got a tremendous thrill after hitting the ball far out into the outfield. The boys were often amazed at my skills in baseball.

In elementary school, I participated in the much-publicized programs developed by President John F. Kennedy's Council on Youth Fitness. I received the first two embroidered patches for the prestigious physical fitness award. In addition, I was the school sit-up champ. I dreamed that some day I would compete in sit-ups against many world competitors for an Olympic gold medal. (Since sit-ups have not yet been designated an Olympic category, I have been able to ease out of that self-imposed expectation.)

Baseball was my favorite sport, but girls did not play baseball in those days. I decided to settle for track. Our school participated in Saturday meets against other schools. Mr. Ben Crouch, Imperial County's athletic coordinator for elementary schools, championed runners' efforts. Whether a red or blue ribbon was handed out, Mr. Crouch was there to shake the athletes' sweaty hands. At our eight grade graduation, I was presented the Best Female Athlete Award. Everyone had expected that I would be chosen for the award. My sister had won the same award the year before.

In my first semester in high school, I began to search for competition in sports. El Rancho High School had successful boys' track and cross-country teams, but no teams for girls. I decided to attend the various meets as a spectator. I checked out the runners to see how many of them were in my classes, and began to ask many questions. Mr. Duane Reidenbach, the athletic director and cross-country and track coach, seemed like an approachable man. The tall, slender coach was a great model of precision and efficiency for his teams. He walked around with a whistle and a stopwatch hanging from his neck. Under one of his muscular arms he always carried a clipboard with a pencil tied to the end.

From a distance, I admired the concise steps Coach Reidenbach took to time his runners for the 880 meters. His long, white fingers clutched the stopwatch as if his life depended on the clicking sound of the seconds passing. As a runner passed the finish mark, the coach used his thumb to stop the clock and then immediately snapped the watch up to his face to examine the time. He always had a word of encouragement for the guys.

I volunteered to help with the team. At first, Coach Reidenbach did not know what to think. He was indifferent to my offer of help, yet knew he could use another set of hands. My persistence paid off. In the fall of my junior year, he asked me to help keep track scores. I worked on the sidelines, but my desire to compete was well-known.

Looking back at this time of my life, I think that Coach Reidenbach knew that I was not physically built to be a serious competitor in track; I did not know this. I was never one to let my dreams die for lack of trying. I was neither slender nor tall, but I kept the impossible dream alive, and Coach Reidenbach never made an effort to dissuade me otherwise.

Eventually, I was the first and only girl on the track team. I could run laps and do all the outdoor exercises required of the boys, but it was difficult being the only girl. In those days, it took a heck of a lot of courage to step on the track with the boys. Girls were expected to be practicing the drill team half-time show or choreographing a modern dance routine. I felt like a zebra in the midst of many giraffes, but the track was for me.

I remember going into the girls' locker room to change into my mandatory "El Rancho High School" gym uniform, powder-blue shorts and a white, short-sleeve cotton blouse. My shoes were thick Keds meant for walking or tennis, not track. After I changed into this feminine running gear, the walk from the girls' gym to the track seemed to be a long mile. My heart pounded at being the only girl out there, but that was not going to stop me either. I downplayed the embarrassment of being the only girl on the track team.

As a new competitor I felt emboldened to challenge the district's assistant superintendent, Mr. Petti, to a mile race. I must have been really serious about sports to try to prove a point to him this way. Like me, Mr. Petti, was short. He did not look like a track star but seemed to be a nice man, and accepted my challenge.

Competition

Many students came out to see us race. Everyone had selected a winner before the race was over. Students and teachers alike were talking about the big winner. I guessed that most students' bets were on Mr. Petti, and figured I had to run hard to beat the odds.

The students and teachers cheered for the underdog, and in the last few feet, I beat Mr. Petti in a photo-finish race. I did not think of this at the time, but perhaps he let me beat him. I want to think that I beat him flat-out. Our school newspaper's headlines focused on the race. For a while, the classrooms were abuzz about the student-vs.-administrator race. Even all these years later, talk about the race still persists.

My aspirations did not stop at the school running track or at our home. I researched the best college track teams and visited sports stores to check out spiked shoes and track clothing. I could see myself in the brightly-colored gear and special spiked shoes.

During El Rancho High School's boys' cross-country and track competitions with other schools, in which I could not participate, I helped clock the boys, keep track scores, and return the hurdles to their positions for the next race. I kept working hard to integrate myself into the scene, even though these games were for boys only.

My best and most loyal friends in high school were the boys on the cross-country team. I admired their perseverance and stamina. They tended to be quiet types, who did not call attention to their athletic efforts. At the end of their races, the stoic runners resembled proud cheetahs relaxing after the chase. The cross-country runners were proud, but took a back seat to the attention-seeking football players.

A special note surprised me a couple of days before graduation. Coach Reidenbach called me to his office. He handed me an envelope and asked that I read it later. I was curious to see the contents, and quietly opened the envelope as I sat in Mr. Reno's chemistry class. To my amazement, the envelope contained a varsity letter — "ER" for El Rancho — inside a plastic bag. A folded piece of white paper was stapled to the bag. I thought this had to be the greatest present a girl could receive. I was so proud of my varsity ER letter, but sad to think that no one would understand the meaning of the effort behind this special memento.

The note, which I have saved to this day, served as a stepping stone to my dreams. It read:

June 1971

Dear Espy,

Thank you for your all your help with the boy's Cross Country and Track teams. You deserved special recognition for your dedication to the track teams. The varsity letter is well-deserved.

Good Luck,
Coach Reidenbach

As my last few months of high school approached, I crafted a small clay statue of Coach Reidenbach holding his clipboard and gave it to him to show my appreciation for his allowing me to be included in the team's efforts.

Two years later, Mr. Reidenbach and his wife, Sharon, were kind enough to accompany me as my official witnesses when I took the U.S. oath of citizenship in San Diego, California.

Later in life, as I pursued a career dominated by men, I knew that my early experiences in sports had helped me understand that not much difference exists between men and women. My strong willingness to take risks in front of others and to stand up to challenges, no matter what, helped pave the way for many positive experiences in my life. To be satisfied with my efforts in the midst of adversity made dreams come true for me. Not being afraid to be around people who were so different in many ways propelled my levels of confidence for future work-force challenging experiences.

My race for success was inspired greatly by my involvement in sports and by mentors and elementary school friends like Antonacio, Frank, Tony, Greg, Oscar, Jerry, Julian, and others who taught me more than they will ever realize. In high school, I qualified for the work-study program to support low-income students. Amazingly, I landed a job with the City of Pico Rivera working in the Parks and Recreation Department. For several years, I kept men's softball stats and helped prepare the fields for the exciting matches. I spent much time observing the men and their behaviors and understanding the timings of their actions during these competitive games. These experiences were unique to me and important to my present environment.

Being competitive is not something that is done alone. No matter what type of competition, it takes an inordinate amount of stamina and determination, with a clear goal to move ahead. Early on, the wings of bamboo provided the first edge of learning the ways of competition and holding on until the goal was accomplished. Most importantly, it takes sturdy support from families and friends, along with a strong belief and trust in one's true and honest actions, to move forward in reaching the desired goals.

Sixteenth of September

1971

I spent most of the summer of 1969 getting to know new friends on Passons Boulevard in Pico Rivera. The city was like many suburbs of Los Angeles, made of up of mostly Mexican-American residents who had been born and raised there. A light wave of immigrants was just beginning to move into Pico.

The pride of being of Mexican descent was evident all over the city. Besides having significant Mexican-American representation on the city council and school board, many businesses were owned by first-, second-, and third-generation Mexicans. The descriptive words "Hispanic" and "Latino" were not common in those days, but the Mexican flag was flown everywhere, along with the U.S. stars and stripes.

The Mexican-American residents of Pico Rivera did not hide their cultural pride. In 1970, in honor of their ancestors, they decided to celebrate the city's first Sixteenth of September Fiesta, in honor of

México's Independence Day. City leaders, agreeing to recognize the positive influence of the culture and heritage of many of Pico Rivera's residents, announced a contest to select a Sixteenth of September queen.

In mid-August, when I stopped at El Rancho High School to pick up my schedule for the new school year, one of the well- known secretaries, Ms. Anita Reyna, told me that the City was looking for young women to nominate for queen of this first-time fiesta. Her comments made no impression on me, until I returned a few days later. Again, Ms. Reyna suggested that I think about competing. It occurred to me that her last name means "queen" in Spanish. Ms. "Queen" wanted me to compete in the queen competition.

Besides Ms. Reyna, classmates encouraged me to consider the opportunity. As usual, I was being pushed out in front of the pack to do something different.

After determining that the contest did not require any high heels, swimsuit or parental involvement, I decided to accept the invitation to participate. I knew they did not have money; therefore I could not ask for that type of support. Besides, my parents would never permit us to wear shorts, in public let alone a swim suit on a run-way for a personality contest! The contestants, I was told, had to speak before the judges. I figured that the speaking part would be the easiest part of the contest. My first speech before judges had been in the third grade, and my English was much better now. My parents were supportive of my school involvement, as long as I handled most of the responsibilities of the event. Our agreement was informal for most school-related social activities. My parents did not understand English and shied away from the public involvement with social functions involving my school or community activities. It was not that they did not want to participate; they were also somewhat embarrassed that they could not speak the English language.

As the contest day drew near, I became worried about what to wear and what to say to the judges. My parents were poor, and I could not bother them for money to help me with this activity. My $1.25-an-hour work-study job at the City Park would have to pay for a new dress for the evening competition.

I asked my father what I should say at the contest. He rarely attended school functions but was filled with ideas and recommendations. "Be proud of whom you are," he said. "Do not think that because you are poor, you can not win," he told me. "Always speak with your heart. No matter whether people are poor or rich, they will know when you are sincere."

My father's constant encouragement was not enough on this occasion. I did not think I had a good chance of winning, since the other girls were long-time, established residents of the area. Nevertheless, I began looking for a dress suitable for the event. In recent months I had become self-conscious about not having the "American Girl" figure. I was short, and my hips seemed too wide. I knew that the other girls would be wearing beautiful dresses, so it was important to find one that would make me feel good about myself.

To my satisfaction, I finally found a dark-purple crêpe dress with long sleeves. The bodice was fitted above the waist, and the crêpe flowed into pleats from the waist down. The dress was appropriate for a nun out of habit, but I felt the beauty of the color and style was perfect to cover up a certain level of embarrassment I had about being in the queen contest. The purple dress was just right in view of the fact that my parents were strict about the amount of skin we showed in public.

I remembered the coronation of the Sixteenth of September queens in our small Mexican village of La Yerbabuena when I was little. Young girls walked behind the queen, holding up her long, white train that extended behind her. On several occasions, as we paraded with the entourage on the cobblestone streets, the spectators tossed what seemed like a ton of confetti on us. I knew that this was going to be something I wanted to do when I was a grown woman. The queens always looked so pretty and secure.

It was my turn to speak in front of judges and answer their questions. Perhaps the part that made my hands perspire the most was the thought of walking across a raised platform, so the audience could look at me. I reminded myself that I would not be the only one doing all of this. Twelve other girls also shared this anxiety.

Finally, the night of the contest arrived. I dressed at my sister's home, as she was to accompany me to the competition. I did not invite my parents, just as I had not done in the past to most school activities. In this case, I thought the contest might offend them. I was glad that some of my high school friends attended the contest. They were funny and gave me great support. My friends tried to give me lots of advice on the contest, but I knew they did not have the courage to stand in front of people and speak.

When we arrived at the elementary school where the contest was being held, my heart fell to my knees when I saw all the other girls in dresses so much more elegant than mine--formal gowns with fancy lace decorations. They looked very pretty and ready for the win. In comparison, I thought my purple crêpe dress looked like Cinderella's rags before her fairy godmother transformed her for the ball. If points were awarded for the contestants' dresses, I was going to fall in last place.

I watched the contestants' mothers, aunts and older sisters fussing with the last-minute details of hair and fancy makeup with bright red lipstick. I wore my long hair straight down, and would not have thought to do otherwise, since my family did not have the resources to send me to a beautician. My NYC Work-Study funds, earned in a work program for underprivileged children, were the only source of income I could spend on this event. However, the excitement of the event made me quickly forget about the things I did not have, and instead I concentrated on my speech and the thoughts that I would convey to the anxious audience.

We were escorted in a group to a classroom to anxiously wait our turns for the individual speeches. After each young woman completed her speech, she was allowed to remain in the cafeteria to watch the contestants who followed. Because my name began with the letter "Z," I was the last one to speak and, therefore, unable to see any of the contestants or listen to any of their prepared speeches.

I was left alone in the classroom, as the next-to-last girl left the room to give her speech. I could feel and hear my heart pound through my purple dress. When my turn came, I was escorted to the cafeteria, where the rest of the contestants were sitting together, waiting anxiously for the nail-biting event to finish. The judges had clipboards with white forms to fill out on each of us. This scene reminded me so much of the feedlot as the young steers moved quickly through the chutes into the waiting truck, as the cowboys pointed to the best and strongest of the stock.

We had been instructed to begin by saying our names and talking a little about our families. I do not remember exactly everything I said, but I recall speaking about my mother and father and our upbringing. I told the judges and the audience how proud I was to be of Mexican descent, and how proud I was of my hard-working parents who did not speak English but wanted us to be the best in school. I told them how much I appreciated the opportunity to represent Pico Rivera as the first Sixteenth of September Queen. Then I quickly repeated what I had said, but this time in Spanish for my sister's benefit. My father's words of advice were in my thoughts.

When I finished, everyone began clapping. I felt that I had done my best performance, but I had no way to compare myself with the other girls, since I had not had the opportunity to see them compete. We waited nervously together, while the judges tallied their scores.

When the third- and second-place winners were finally announced, I decided I had not done a great job. I should have worked harder on my speech and carefully written down more specific thoughts. But then the winner was announced. "Espy Zendejas!" I heard announced over the microphone. I sat for a few seconds until another contestant woke me up from my daze.

Suddenly, the purple dress became the perfect dress, and my father's inspiring and sincere words had helped me to win the competition. Roses were handed to me, just like in the real Miss America contest. A simple but pretty crown decorated my plain hairstyle. A large ribbon bearing my title crossed from my shoulder to my waist.

What a great evening! My arms were filled with gifts, and lipstick was all over my cheeks from the many women who wished me well. My sister was elated, to say the least. She had great news to tell her friends at the local Mattel Toy Factory where she worked.

During September, I attended many functions and visited with many people. My sister made me a white taffeta (a type of dressy fabric) dress with shiny silver decorations to wear for these occasions. I know in my heart that she felt sad that my parents could not afford to buy me fancy, prom-style dresses for this notable occasion. Special photos were taken of me in this homemade dress, posed in front of a red, green, and white ribbon representing the Mexican flag. My brother Hector drove me downtown to find a dress for the Sixteenth of September Fiesta. He wanted me to look nice in front of all the dignitaries. In the shopping area of *La Placita* (shopping area in Los Angeles), we found a black velvet dress with colorful sequins and Mexican designs on the skirt and blouse.

On September 17,[th] the local newspapers ran photos of the proud Mexican-American girl next to Pico Rivera's city leaders. As a young adult, this was one of the few moments that I have been part of where I have felt our culture was embraced on a personal level. How proud my parents must also have been in their own humble way!

My *Familia*

2005

It has been the enduring, unconditional love of our parents and their unquestionable determination for us to have a better life than what was promised in our native México that enabled us to reach our goals, dreams and more. My parents were the brave ones in our family. They dared to venture into the unknown world of America, the plentiful. Without much money or the knowledge of the language, our parents set out to serve others in low-wage jobs in order to achieve the American dream for our good.

It was assumed that the only thing needed by immigrants in America was a Mexican broom. There was so much money on the streets of the United States that a broom could quickly sweep the dollars into the pockets of the starving immigrants. We never caught sight of the scattering of dollars on the streets of the United States. Instead, it was all related to how hard the family members wanted to work that would eventually produce the desired benefits. Indeed, our voyage to the United States has been one of faith, hard work and a determined, positive spirit. It has been almost forty-five years since we first arrived in California's Imperial Valley, and not a day goes by without our recognizing the unselfish sacrifices made by our parents on our behalf.

The *alas de carrizo* (wings of bamboo) became powerful elements of my life from various points of view. The *alas de carrizo* have taken me and my family to far-away places. Everyone should find their own *alas de carrizo* so that they may be taken to a world of optimism and motivation to accomplish whatever hopes and dreams they may have. The humble wings of bamboo that were tightly arranged behind my back on special religious occasions in our native México proved to be an energetic force in the life-long impetus.

Every family has many warm and loving stories to share. Our family shares many beautiful experiences of being raised in two countries with two languages by a set of loving and caring parents. We continue to cherish being part of a family that believes in hard work, determination and no excuses. Our parents did a magnificent job raising nine of us during a time of limited resources and limited choices. For all of their work, the outcome has been a relatively well-adjusted family. Our parents offered us what money can not buy: love.

Not all the experiences growing up in different cultures and languages were pleasant or agreeable, but all offered learning opportunities and a whole lot of humility. Our parents' supportive ways and emotional support guided us through our new venture in a different country and through a difficult time learning a new language. Our parents always had a calming way of dealing with difficult issues. Our dear parents wanted us to believe in ourselves first before expecting others to believe in us. We were taught to look for the peaceful side of people and situations

Any real impediments during our journey were smoothed over by our parents' attentive and compassionate ways. They provided a sensible and seamless transition from México to the United States in their own special ways. Failure was not an option in their plans for us. Our parents kept the fire in our stomachs lighted, creating an indisputable hunger to succeed. Thanks to our parents, we continued to respect and value the cultural roots of our birthplace and value the cultural enrichment of our current, diverse communities.

Most importantly, I know that these stories provide a daring and compassionate glimpse of our past. In some ways, these childhood stories provide a peek into our family and our efforts to succeed in order to make our parents proud. I am confident that these stories will serve to inspire the young and old of many lands and many lan-guages. These are the similar stories of many immigrants who have made difficult decisions and have changed their own family's history in courageous and meaningful ways.

In closing *Wings of Bamboo*, I would like to reintroduce my parents and siblings in 2005. I am proud of all my brothers and sisters for what they have accomplished and thankful to my parents for never giving up on any of us throughout the extraordinary times. They offered discipline when needed, love when yearned-for and kindness when it was desperately needed. My parents were true and faithful in accepting the awe-inspiring challenges of raising nine very different children in a variety of economical and distressed conditions.

Regretfully, many that see success cannot look beyond the present. All of my siblings have struggled to get to where they are today. Long hours, tears and many uncounted sacrifices are not easy to reconstruct for the benefit of those that want to learn of our family's efforts at getting ahead. Some are still struggling to make ends meet and to see that their families succeed. My brothers' and sisters' successes can be summed up into three words: hard, determined work!

When we were very young, we did not have much, and the fear of losing what we had was not a major concern. When we were in the United States, my parent's worries were to make enough to feed the family and to pay the basic bills. Looking back, being poor was so much more simple-or perhaps less complicated? The worries and challenges of today are multiple and more complex.

As the youngest child of the family of nine, I have been following the footprints and learning from the experiences left for me by my siblings and parents. I hope that I can leave behind a visible and positive footpath for other family members and generations to follow. My family has inspired a willingness to take risks and to appreciate the lessons of the falls that come with the unknown and from mistakes made along the way. We did not have much while growing up, except the love of our two parents and a strong value of work and play.

On January 31, 2001, the rosary and prayer as we once knew it would never be the same after the passing of our dear mother. This family's symphony of prayer had lost its beloved orchestra director. Yet, the echo of our mother's voice, and her beliefs in the strength and peace from prayer, fondly planted in our hearts, will forever continue to propel the love and spirit of our large family. The singing of "*Adios Reyna Del Cielo, Madre del Salvador, Adios O Madre Mia, Adios, Adios, Adios*" was drowned by the tears and thickness of the vocal cords at the passing of our mother. My mother instilled in us the basic foundation and determination to live and succeed. Through her character, she injected in us a great deal of internal fortitude to overcome the many challenges that life hands out to all. Yet at the same time, she implored that we remain humble and close to the people and the Mother earth.

She demonstrated her great pride and distinct joy in being our mother and our guide during both the fun and the difficult periods of growing up to adulthood. For many years, she thoughtfully served and patronized our needs. For this and more, my father continues to honor the woman that raised his nine children in a humble and poor environment.

After my father retired from his last job as a crop irrigator in the Imperial Valley, he and my mother returned to our birthplace in Michoacán, México. His first of many projects was tearing down the old, adobe mud home and rebuilding it with more durable cement-block material. He added enough rooms for the entire family, including grandchildren. To my mother's delight, he made sure two fully equipped kitchens were available for her delicious recipes.

My father still lives in México. He is a wise man, with much gusto and a strong spirit for life. He continues to fill our thoughts with colorful and poetic comments about family life, nature and politics. He often reminds us of his growing up in a very poor environment. He is quick to note that he slept many a night under a "thousand-star" hotel, simply stating that he slept under the Mexican skies as a child during the times he guarded the corn crop from the deer, coyotes and other corn-loving animals. He believes that while he was poor, his sleeping quarters were better than today's "five- star" accommodations. To this day, he firmly believes that the best religion in the world is that of "peace."

Despite his love of life and endless energy, my father's 92-year-old fragile body is beginning to slow down. We are all amazed as he continues to be a voracious reader. With a thick magnifying glass, he slowly inches his way across the black ink lines of English or Spanish newspapers. No matter what, he continues to read the distorted words of the print. Of the entire family, he probably can outsmart most everyone with his knowledge on current events and world politics.

His ears have slowly shut him off from the familiar chatter and laughter of the family members. He no longer can hear with clarity the fine tunes from the *Banda de Zirahuen* (favorite Tarascan Indigenous group of musicians from the Lake of Zirahuen in Michoacán, México) music or the infectious laughter emanating from Blanca's strong lungs. The entire family now raises the voice decibels when speaking to him in person or over the long-distance telephone calls.

Most recently, my father's teeth have bitten into enough corn and chewed enough tortillas. Thanks to skillful dental support, he will receive a new set of white teeth. We all know that he will show everyone his new tools by smiling, laughing and repeating his most memorable stories one-hundred times over. Most importantly, his will to live and his positive character are important factors in his energetic personality. He reminds us that he is now on the "over-time" clock of life.

The frequency of his trips to the corn *milpa* in the green hills of the mountains has decreased in recent years. It is not as easy for him to walk up and down the volcanic, stone-filled hills as it once was only a few years back. My father continues to plant a smaller crop of corn and beans to show us that everything is still possible. He wants us to continue to believe in hard work and the good of the harvest of the dedicated labor. At his age, his skillful use of words to describe events and tell stories continues to amaze all of us. His intellect has been regarded as sharp and witty by his friends and relatives. He is seemingly quite content as he watches the large, happy family mingle at gatherings, knowing that both he and my mother co-authored the existence of this proud family.

In recent years, my father has had his share of challenges. In January 2000, he was trampled by a large cow and seriously injured on both arms. The hooves of the large animal were imprinted on his forearms and hands, as large, open and serious wounds. Infection was quickly crawling below the surface of his wounds. The family agreed to have him see a hand specialist in Indianapolis, Indiana the very next day. Dr. Hasting and his team of medical hand experts provided remarkable care and compassion for my father's delicate case.

His willpower to return home as quickly as possible was evident as he bid farewell to my mother. He emphatically and lovingly told her that he would return soon. It was the first time in my entire life that I had seen such deep love and devotion between two individuals. If life allowed us to freeze certain moments in time, this moment would be a keeper. I wished I had the capability of reconstructing the reality of this exchange to share with other family members.

In Indianapolis, the growing infection on his hands was successfully removed after several painful surgeries. It was excruciating to watch him dip his hands in the cleansing chlorinated water, as his tears rolled off his cheeks, without complaining. It became evident to me that it was easier to watch young children cry than to watch your own parents suffer and cry out from physical pain. After many months of self-directed therapy, my father returned to planting his yearly crop of corn, beans and squash. After several months of painstaking efforts to cleanse the layers of old skin to make room for the new, my father regained most of the use of his hands. After this major incident, his hands have lost much of their strength, but he is able to use them.

Like the rest of us, my father dearly misses my mother. My father now spends much time sharing my mother's stories to keep her spirit alive. My mother was the one who led in prayer and now, it is my father who spends significant time praying for all of us. In 2001, my father and the four girls traveled to Rome to pay special tribute to my mother's dedication and respect for prayer and the Pope. For that matter, it was a bitter-sweet trip.

My father is so proud of America. He is grateful for the opportunities that this land offered him and his family with welcoming arms. To his great pride, my father's ranch property, located on the green hills, was named "Calipatria, 92233" after the town and zip code that witnessed our early progress in the United States.

My brothers and sisters are all contributing members of their own communities in their special ways. All of my brothers and sisters, along with their spouses or significant others, are now leading their own families and welcoming new their new generations. There are grandchildren, great-grandchildren and great-great-grandchildren. In all, our family numbers over one hundred and twenty individuals. I suppose we would have to rent an entire hotel to host a family gathering.

María Elena, the eldest, now lives in Thousand Oaks, California, with her husband, Tommy. She continues to be devoted to prayer. Her strong, charismatic attitude is well-regarded. Her sharp eyes and observant personality have not changed to this date. She has taken up some of my mother's passion for the rosary and prayer. My oldest sister has always held a special place for me. She has been one of my best public relations spokespersons, when it comes to telling my stories about our successful efforts.

Moreover, she usually carries a full portfolio of pictures and certificates to show the best side of family members. On any given day, María Elena, like magic, can pull a 1971 newspaper clipping from Pico Rivera, California, during my days in high school. Her latest showing has been the folded U.S. Certificate of Naturalization, pledging her allegiance to the United States of America. On a sad note, she also will share pictures of her departed son, Tommy Jr. She inherited my father's hunger for conversation, no matter what time of the day. I am ever grateful to her and her husband for hosting us during my high school years in El Rancho.

Years ago, María Elena was diagnosed with the rare parasite infection Trichinosis. She met this medical challenge with bravery and determination. She has survived several delicate brain surgeries, giving everyone much hope and appreciation for life.

After her surgeries, she has rebounded into a normal, life-loving and happy individual.

María Elena and Tommy Reyes have three grown children including Joanne, Sergio and Mariann. In the mid-eighties Tommy Jr. was involved in a fatal accident. No one knows the pain and gravity of a son or daughter's passing except for those that have experienced the dreadful, unexpected outcome. It is so true that in life of a constant order, parents should not bury their own children. As a family, we have all mourned the passing of our kind and gentle nephew. María Elena enjoys the company of her grandchildren.

María Elena ingratiates herself with her neighbors and friends. Her amiable attitude is well regarded by those around her. "My mother is an extremely popular person around our community because of her loving and kind ways with people. My mother is always seeking the best through prayer for her children and her family. She has been a faithful companion to our father. We have been fortunate to have such a supportive and loving mother," stated her son Sergio.

Gustavo recently moved back to the Imperial Valley with his second wife and youngest child. His love of horses continues to light his fire and keep his passion alive. His expertise in raising horses is second to none. The sweet smell of horse and hay follows Gustavo like a kindred spirit. In the words of his eldest daughter, Mari, "My father taught me to ride horses and when thrown off, he wanted me to get up, as we should in real life after a fall. He always wanted me to forget about the fall and concentrate on the rest of the ride, as in real life." Gustavo has six children, including five daughters and one son— María, Cuca, Estela, Teresa, Gustavo and Victoria.

Rodo resides in the outskirts of Niland, California. He moved into the same house that once burned down on Mother's Day in 1974. He loves and enjoys the country setting. He continues to work as a migrant, even though all his nine children discourage him from such hard, laborious work. His deep wrinkles show the tough and sun-drenched road he has had to follow. Today, Rodo is semi-retired but continues to work with his hands, picking citrus for a living and raising goats as a hobby.

His tough, calloused hands are indicative of the hard work and his constant connection that he has with the fertile land. I love to touch his hands, as they remind me of the work and labor that brought us to America. He has a special way with plants, growing seedlings into fruited trees, or blossoming plants in a short time. He also has a special talent for plant grafting. His other hobby is singing. He loves to sing at all family gathering.

Rodo has the largest number of children in our close-knit family-- nine. His eldest child, Silvino, is followed by Elia Irma, María Monica, Rodolfo, Felipe de Jesus, Jose Antonio, Patricia, Diego and Cesar. "My father was an extremely responsible man during our growing-up years. He always managed to help everyone out.

My father encouraged me to stay in school. Early on, he taught me
the first lessons of math. His simple ways of adding numbers
together enlightened the rest of my math career," stated his first
son, Silvino.

My sister Cuca served as my mother's house-nurse and now is
helping our aging father with his daily routines. She has taken a
temporary family leave from the convent to provide the 24/7 care
needed for our motivated father. Cuca and my father reside most
of the year in La Yerbabuena, Michoacán, México. She currently
manages our large home, making all of us feel welcome to recon-
nect with our Mexican rural roots. At the point when my father
passes, she will return to her normal responsibilities as a nun with
the order of the Holy Family in Michoacán.

Today, she wears a less formal religious habit. She helps the small
town with the religious responsibilities. She is often called upon
to pray for the sick and to help in medical emergencies. She gets
called to tend to the dying in preparing the bodies for the final
blessings.

She continues to keep our Catholic faith and home altar nicely
decorated for the family and friends in La Yerbabuena, Michoacán.
"Whenever we traveled to México, my *tía* (aunt) Cuca was there for
all of us. She helped us with our preparation for the required first
communion. Thanks to my *tía*, my first communion was a great
success and a happy celebration with all the nuns in her convent.
She stitched a white habit for my communion dress and took many

memorable pictures at the convent," stated Baleria, my daughter. Cuca is the respected in-house expert on all religious ceremonies and celebrations. Cuca is called whenever a questions arises involving the church or religious events.

Alfonso is still working with cattle and cow chips. He has dedicated all his life to the cattle business in Imperial Valley. With the exception of a short career as a fancy waiter in a Los Angeles restaurant, he has worked in the cattle business ever since we arrived in the Imperial Valley. He has been through the good and the bad times of the cattle industry. In addition, he has gained a wealth of knowledge on medical care in tending to the sick animals. He never attended school but is proud of the fact that he learned on-the-job the skills and knowledge needed to care for the frail, four-legged animals. He still believes that the smell of manure is the smell of pure gold. Alfonso is also dedicating more time to raising and caring for his fidgety goats.

To honor his fine dedication and love for the cattle industry, in November 2004, Alfonso was named one of several celebrity Grand Marshals for the Cattle Call Parade and Rodeo in Brawley, California. His gracious smile paraded down the streets of Brawley, showing off his contagious personality, proudly representing the modern cowboy of today.

Alfonso has six grown children: Sylvia, Peter, Tony, Jaime, Gustavo and Frances. Most importantly, Alfonso will be found at every family gathering, encouraging the party and festive occasion, whether he is invited or not. To this day he goes out on the dance floor to show all the young family members a few prized dancing steps and gentle twists of the legs and hips, with the sound of the mariachi or band music playing in the background. His youthful, spirited moves on the dance floor bring smiles from all watching his older body move with unmeasured grace. He has a way of captivating the attention of all around him. The happy-go-lucky brother has given us many great memories to pass on to future generations.

"To this date my father keeps insisting that we must remember who we are and where we came from. He regularly reminds us to make sure that we take care of the family and to respect our elders in the most reverend manner. My father's great sense of humor has rubbed off on all of us," said Frances, his youngest daughter. Alfonso takes much pleasure and joy in telling the story of the cherished Christmas present he prepared for me during one of our first holiday seasons in the United States. He resides with his wife on the outskirts of Calipatria, California.

Luis currently is a key partner in a successful hardware business store in Calipatria. His other partners are his three sons and daughter. Luis and his wife, Eileen, reside surrounded by their four children and grandchildren. The family business satisfies the hardware needs of the local farmers and community. Luis is still battling the effects of injuries suffered while serving in the military during the Vietnam War. He has recently gone through additional medical attention for war-related consequences. No matter what, his positive attitude and courage will continue to make him strong. He has inherited much of my father's way of looking at life with a positive and prosperous attitude.

His continued good nature and helping spirit have gained him many friends and loyal clients. Luis continues to inspire his family and community through his hard work. His son Chris notes, "My father has instilled in us a strong work ethic. He also taught us to be true to ourselves in doing what is right, even if it ruffles some feathers." Luis and his three sons, Chris, Jeff and Moses, manage the Zendejas Hardware Store in Calipatria. Patricia, the youngest of the family, is currently serving in the military.

Hector has proven his sharp skills at growing needed crops as a custom farmer. He grows alfalfa, cotton, sugar beets and on occasions takes on special requests for specialized crops that grow well in the hot summers and mild winters of Imperial Valley. The one-man operation requires much of his time during the day and night, watching and tending his crops and ensuring that they get the required amount of water. The day is never too long for his work and dedication to agriculture. Hector has dedicated most of his life to working with the fertile grounds of his beloved Imperial Valley. He began working with Don Cannon in the sixties. Hector is now a well-respected farmer in the southern end of Imperial County. He also served in the Army, having been stationed in Germany. He recently became a proud United States citizen.

Hector's jokes and comical tactics are still being enjoyed by the family. His ways with his friends have gained him much respect and admiration. His friends enjoy his company very much. "My father has a special way with people. He is able to make friends easily. While we were growing up, my father taught us to work with the highest levels of expectations," stated his son Arcy.

Hector is the proud father of two boys, Arcy and Gabby and several grandchildren. Lately, he has taken on other hobbies with goats and horses. He loves the country and the fresh-air environment.

Blanca is a successful real estate agent in Ventura County. She probably is known in the family for the most careers undertaken within a span of twenty-some years. She went from store clerk, frosty cone-maker, home decorator, beautician to real estate agent. When we were growing up, she had it in her heart to become a stewardess. Unfortunately, at the time, her Mexican figure did not match with the airline's perfect and stringent stewardess profile. Later on, she shifted her career aspirations and focused on becoming a nurse. She even volunteered as a candy striper in a local hospital, wearing a pretty white and red striped uniform.

She continues to serve her three children with a loving dedication and is often sought by younger members of the large family seeking advice on life's challenges and opportunities. Blanca continues to be the soothing voice for me but, more importantly, has become the peaceful voice of the rest of the family. Her three children have referred to her as a "strong person, a determined individual" in light of the many obstacles and challenges she has faced. "My mother raised the three of us in a positive environment, despite the fact that she raised us as a single parent. We were a very happy family, surrounded by cousins and friends," her son Michael proudly stated.

Her favorite sport is shopping. She has a way of stretching the dollar unlike anyone else I know. Her laughter is probably the best-known and loudest at all family gatherings. Her spirit of giving is central to her everyday living. Blanca has three grown children: Lisa, Michelle and Michael.

The nine children of Silvino and María Zendejas come together to celebrate birthdays, weddings and fiestas in La Yerbabuena, Michoacán, México. We also come together to honor those that have left our presence to enter another world. The young nieces and nephews have grown to be caring parents and prosperous citizens. The great-grandchildren are beginning to wed and to have children of their own. We are proud of the five generations of the humble and loving family of Silvino and María Zendejas.

Success in our family was not how much money was earned or how many honors or certificates were presented to us. Our parents measured our accomplishments by the fortitude of our character and the determination of our will. In our family it was more about being kind and caring to family, relatives and friends.

Finally, I know that that María Elena, Gustavo, Rodolfo, Cuca, Alfonso, Luis, Hector, Blanca and I have much to thank our parents, as they made life easier for all of us during the tough times. Our parents, in their own ways taught us about kindness, love and hard work. They taught right from wrong. They made a lasting impression on our souls and fundamental ways of being. Now, we must strive to make life a better place for our own children, family and future generations!

Finale

The *Wings of Bamboo* is a collection of a cherished childhood stories that have made an impact on my life. These stories take place during a time of monumental change and challenge for all of us. There are still many stories of México, California, family and friends that need to be told. Yet to be told are stories of my experiences while in El Rancho High School, Imperial Valley College and the rest of my post-secondary education. The childhood stories in *Wings of Bamboo* are the pleasant stories of growing up. I am also certain that many details were left unnoted either because I did not remember or because I was too involved in other aspects of growing up at the time of the story.

I hope that these stories will inspire generations of young adults to work hard to achieve their dreams by seeking those elements that will help them succeed. For me, my dear grandparents, my parents and siblings played supportive roles to my growing up. I realize that our children will not have to work as hard as our parents or our grandparents. Life in general is much easier today in some respects and more complicated in others. Above all, however, I firmly believe that life waits for those that aspire to live to achieve.

About the Author

Esperanza Zendejas attended Niland Elementary School and El Rancho High School. She graduated from Imperial Valley Community College, San Diego State University, University of San Diego and Stanford University. She has a bachelor's degree in Liberal Arts, a master's degree in Counseling and a Doctor of Education Degree from Stanford University. She has been a teacher, counselor, principal, central office administrator and school superintendent. Currently, Esperanza is the superintendent of East Side Union High School District in San Jose, California.

In 1995, Esperanza and John Fox married in Indianapolis, Indiana. Esperanza and her husband reside in California. They have three grown children; Baleria is a teacher in Brownsville, Texas, Xchel is a junior at Arizona State University in Tempe, and Angela is a sophomore at Indiana University in Bloomington.

Esperanza has also published two novels, *The Tame Cactus* and *Infallibility*, about brave and determined women overcoming challenging obstacles. Esperanza is currently completing her fourth book, *Chicken Mole.*

Esperanza continues to provide enthusiastic and motivating keynote addresses throughout the United States and Mexico. As a ventriloquist, she entertains children of all ages with her sidekick, Kiko.